BRUISED

AMULET BOOKS • NEW YORK

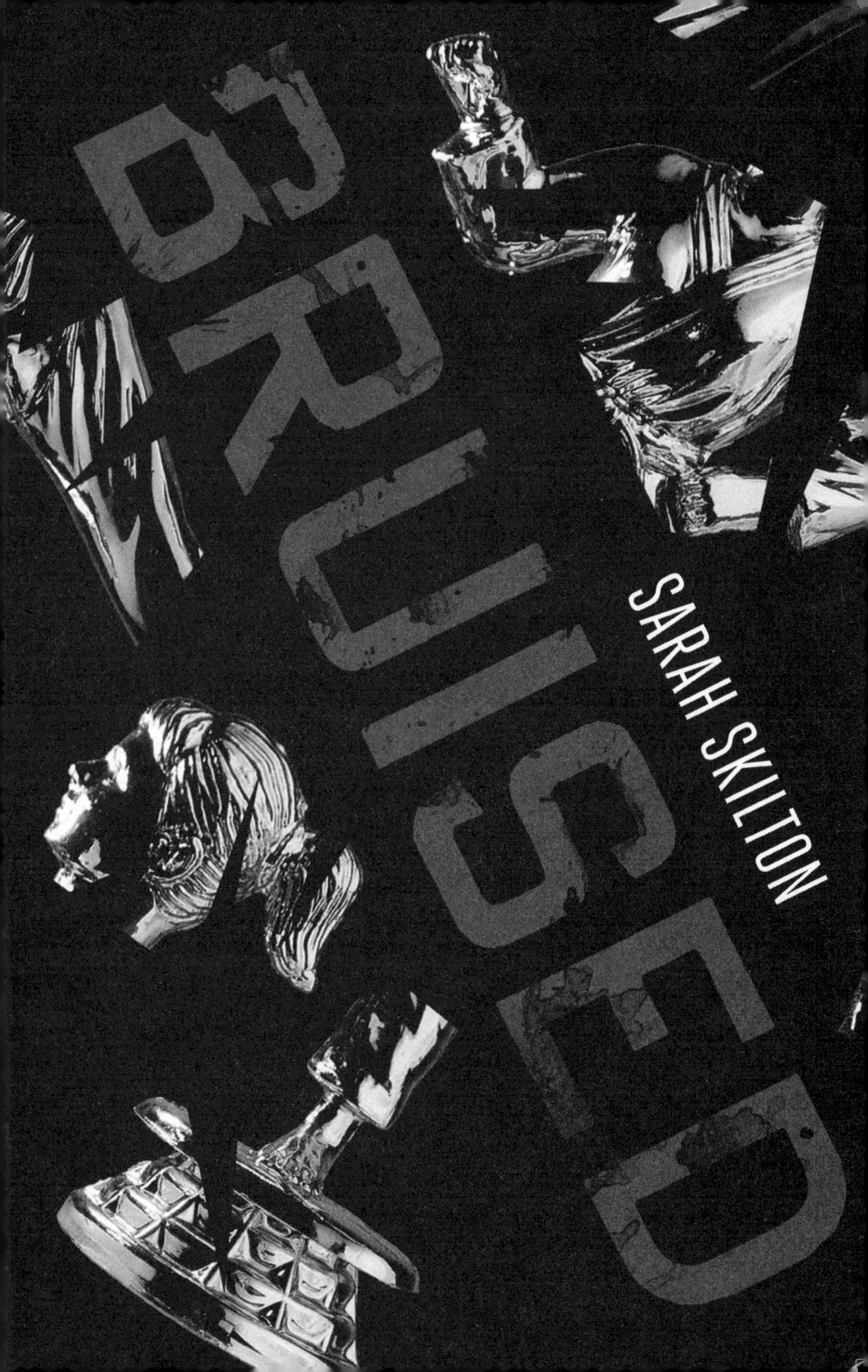
BRUISED
SARAH SKILTON

PUBLISHER'S NOTE: This is a work of fiction. Names, characters, places, and incidents are either the product of the author's imagination or are used fictitiously, and any resemblance to actual persons, living or dead, business establishments, events, or locales is entirely coincidental.

The Library of Congress has catalogued the hardcover edition of this book as follows:

Skilton, Sarah.
Bruised / by Sarah Skilton.
pages cm
Summary: When she freezes during a hold-up at the local diner, sixteen-year-old Imogen, who always believed that her black belt in Tae Kwan Do made her better than everyone else, has to rebuild her life, including her relationship with her family and with a certain boy.
ISBN 978-1-4197-0387-4
[1. Tae kwon do—Fiction. 2. Martial arts—Fiction.
3. Self-perception—Fiction.] I. Title.
PZ7.S6267Br 2013
[Fic]—dc23
2012042801

ISBN for this edition: 978-1-4197-1017-9

Book design by Maria T. Middleton

Printed and bound in U.S.A.
10 9 8 7 6 5 4 3 2 1

115 West 18th Street
New York, NY 10011
www.abramsbooks.com

FOR JOE

1

BY THE TIME MY BROTHER ARRIVES, HE CAN'T GET TO ME.

The cops have barricaded the diner—two blocks in all directions. Blood and worse coats my hair, my face, and my clothes, sticking to me like chunks of blackberry jam. They had to cut me out of my shirt, but since they can't cut me out of my skin, I don't see how I'll ever be clean.

It took me six years to get my black belt.

Two fifty-five-minute classes every Monday and Wednesday after school, plus Friday night sparring and Saturday morning demo-team practice. Two belt tests per year, spring and fall, like a pendulum swinging ever higher.

I memorized the colors, chanted them to myself in bed at night. The walls of the *dojang* were white except for a section at the front of the room, underneath the Korean and American flags, where a brightly painted chart in the shape of a ladder, one fat brick per color, reached up to the ceiling. As if I'd ever forget.

White belt, yellow belt, orange belt, purple belt, green belt, light blue belt, dark blue belt, red belt, red with black stripe, brown belt, brown with black stripe, black belt.

And guess what black is? Hint: It's not the end. It's not the highest level, not even close. Black belt means now you get to start. *Now you get to learn martial arts.* You're back at the beginning: first degree. There are twelve degrees, and each one takes years and years to achieve, maybe even a decade. Only like five people in the world are twelfth-degree black belts, and they're ancient and live on top of mountains and stuff.

My instructor, Grandmaster Huan, is a ninth degree. Chief Master Paulson is a fourth degree. I was the first female to earn a black belt at my school, and the youngest.

I've heard that in Korea there are no colors. You start out as a white belt, and then one day your instructor decides you're a black belt. No rhyme, no reason. At least, none that you'd understand. There's no guarantee you'll be good enough, and no set time when they have to promote you. You have to prove yourself. You have to earn it beyond a doubt.

You have to accept that it might never happen.

But when all those Korean masters came to the United States, they added colors in order to teach and make a living, because they *knew* American kids wouldn't be able to stand working hard without anything to show for it. They *knew* American kids couldn't handle waiting for something that might never come. Most of all, they knew American parents wanted their monthly checks to translate into evidence that their kid was making progress, that all the yelling and kicking and punching in formation had a point.

My black belt wasn't the end, and it wasn't the beginning.

It doesn't represent six years of hard work, constant practice, anxiety attacks on test day, stacks of certificates, a cabinet full of trophies, sweat, pain, and elation—or Friday nights spent sparring while my friends went to the movies.

My black belt represents everything I could've done and everything I didn't do, the only time it really mattered.

GRETCHEN'S IN THE BATHROOM WHEN THE GUNMAN comes in.

Everyone else has gone home after tossing a bunch of crumpled bills on the table, saying good night and how they hope they'll see me tomorrow at the homecoming game. They were just being nice; Gretchen and the rest of her senior friends only invited me out because my older brother, Hunter, had to work, and she's only waiting around so she can grill me privately about whether he's seeing anyone.

If he is, he'll be done in an hour.

That's how long it took him to "date" Shelly Eppes, who was my best friend until three weeks ago.

I'm not going to say that, though.

No one's in the diner except the cashier and me. The table's been cleared and wiped down, but there are still bits of hash browns stuck to the corner of the lamination or whatever it is and some packets of ketchup scattered around. They were about to close, but Gretchen asked if she could use the bathroom first, so that's where she is when the gunman comes in, all twitchy and frenetic, with a black ski mask, long tangled hair, and a scruffy coat.

I see him from my position in the corner booth, but he doesn't know I'm there. I'm not close to the windows, so he must not have seen me when he was outside, deciding whether to come in. I see the bright silver glint of a gun in his hand, harsh and fake looking under the fluorescent lights. For a split second, everything seems unreal, like I've wandered onto the set of a horror film. For a split second, I don't register what's going on.

And then I get under the table.

I tuck my knees under my chin and wrap my arms around my legs until I'm a compact little ball. My heart bashes itself against the bars of my rib cage, trying to stage a prison break.

The table legs feel like widely spaced tree trunks in a field, leaving me exposed, so I contract further. I pull my breath in like I'm shoving and cramming it into a drawer that's already full, and then I lock the drawer before anything spills out.

That's when I notice someone else is there, under a different table, across the aisle. He's crouched the same way as me, he looks about my age, and he's got dark hair and dark eyes.

Slowly, slowly his index finger comes up to his lips. *Shh . . .*

I nod, never breaking eye contact. We don't blink because if we blink the other person might disappear, and then we'll be all alone.

My heart slams so hard I swear it's going to leave my body behind. (Take me with you.) My breath tumbles out in little puffs I fight to suppress.

Above us, the cashier argues with the gunman.

"What the hell are you doing, Daryl?" She sounds annoyed, not frightened.

"Just empty the register," he yells back. "*Shut up.*"

"What the hell?" she says.

Please don't argue, I think, and I know my friend under the other table is thinking the same thing.

There's more yelling, and then a horrible noise, like a scream, but muffled. Worse than a scream, because we can't tell what's going on.

My friend and I look into each other's eyes and try to block out the fact that it sounds like the gunman has whipped the cashier across her face with the butt of his gun. It sounds like she's choking on teeth and blood. It sounds like she's pleading for her life. A high-pitched moan rolls toward us, piercing my eardrums.

It's horrible, the drawn-out moan, but it means she's still alive.

Please do as he says and maybe he'll go away and you'll be all right.

I've never looked directly into someone else's eyes for this long before. Definitely not a guy's. It would be weird under other circumstances. As long as we're looking at each other, though, we have hope. If the gunman comes near our section, he won't be able to get both of us. One of us will help the other. I know this in my muscles and tendons, which are poised, taut, alert. I know this in the snapping valves of my heart, trying to dislodge from my chest.

I think about Gretchen, willing her to stay in the bathroom, guilty that I haven't thought about her before now. Oh God, she has a bunch of little sisters. I think she's the oldest of five. She's like a nanny crossed with a drill sergeant, because she's used to herding groups of people. Even her friends tonight seemed to agree that sitting back and letting her take charge—of ordering appetizers for the table, deciding how to split the bill, figuring out how everyone should get home—was for the best. There was this sense that, with Gretchen around, things would get done and fun would be had.

Oh God. Let her be safe.

I don't realize she's already called the cops from her cell phone.

All I did was hide.

All I did was hide.

I don't remember what happens next.

There's a wall around that memory I can't climb.

So I'm gonna think about the shoes on my friend under the table. He's wearing clean, bright white sneakers, the kind hip-hop artists wear. They look brand-new. They're perfectly white all over, the laces and logo and sole, like they've been dipped in creamy vanilla, and then they're red because that's what happens next, and I can't—I don't—I don't *want* to remember it.

But neither of us is injured, which is more than the cashier can say; and neither of us is killed, which is more than the gunman can say.

When the cops finally cut me out of my clothes, which are weighing me down like thick red tar, all I can think is, *Who will pay for this shirt? Who will pay for these jeans?*

I rock back and forth and calculate their cost.

"I don't care if you never speak to me again," Hunter says at 3 a.m., kneeling by the side of my bed like he's praying. He's not allowed in my room anymore, but he crept in after we got home, after the cops let me go. "Imogen, I'm so glad you're *safe.*"

His voice quivers on the last word, like he's twelve, and for a second his sobbing reminds me of the cashier, all woeful and pleading. I picture a cat on a windowsill, begging for scraps, not realizing the house is empty because everyone's moved away.

3

WHEN I THINK OF BEFORE, I THINK OF ALL THE COLORS.

The bright white cotton of my Tae Kwon Do uniform.

The ruby-red strawberry smoothies I chugged at breakfast, straight out of the blender, so fast the juice dripped down my chin, so sweet and pure. The tiny seeds caught in my teeth.

Closing up Glenview Martial Arts for the night under an orchid-pink sky streaked with orange like the sun's been smeared by a finger-painting deity, digging his hands in, getting them wet.

I remember the summer: Fireworks on the Fourth of July. Sparklers igniting in fountain-shocks of yellow. Ashy smoke and streamers.

The clear blue chlorinated sheen of the Glenview community pool, where Hannah and DJ worked the concession stand, selling pizza, 7Up, and frozen Charleston Chews. During breaks, my friends would lie out, perfecting their tans. At night they went on double dates with the lifeguards.

They thought about love.

I did, too, but in a different way. For me, it wasn't about finding the perfect guy.

For me, it was about teaching.

In August, Grandmaster Huan ran a three-week self-defense summer camp for kids, in the hope they'd join Glenview Martial Arts for the fall session. This year he asked me to help out.

To get my black belt, I had to assistant-teach sixty hours of beginner and sixty hours of intermediate classes. Teaching makes you better, because in order to explain something to someone else, you have to know it cold.

The camp kids made me nervous, though. Compared with my regular crew, the August kids were prisoners from the gen-pop, scary little brace-faced terrors, dropped off by parents in desperate need of an afternoon cocktail. These kids didn't know to take off their shoes and sit quietly in the hall while the previous class finished up. They didn't know how to bow or in what order to bow. They didn't know the Children's Home Rules or Five Tenets of Tae Kwon Do.

Would they "respect ma authoritay" (as Cartman would

say) or laugh at my attempts to control them? They probably had no idea how old I was. Sixteen? Twenty? Forty-five?

I couldn't let them down; it was my responsibility to demonstrate proper technique.

There was this one new girl, Taylor, who was about to enter sixth grade. She had so much heart, and she cracked me up because she *kiyap*'ed (yelled) louder than anyone else when she kicked, but always a split second too late, like she'd almost forgotten to do it. She had trouble with blocks and counterstrikes because she didn't like getting in other people's space, especially boys' space. Most girls don't, and I wanted to change that.

Her long straggly hair whipped her in the face when she punched. I showed her how to braid it and pin it underneath, all tidy and sneaky, and then I made it my mission to turn her into a fearless fighter.

"Let's say you're at a U of I party, having fun, until a drunk frat boy corners you against the wall," I said. I'd seen the U of I sticker on her mom's car.

Taylor smiled shyly and ducked her head.

I grabbed the collar of her *dobuk* (uniform) and pretended to slam her against the wall.

She twisted, anxious to pull away, but I held fast. "That'll just make it worse. He's bigger and stronger than you."

Taylor was frustrated. "So what do I do?"

"You have to pull him toward you."

I placed Taylor's hands around my wrists. "Pull me in closer."

"But I don't *want* him to come closer." She grimaced.

"I know, it's weird and it doesn't seem logical, but it's what he's least expecting, right? If you pull him in, that throws him off-balance mentally *and* physically, and you can get the upper hand."

She nodded, but the way her throat moved, I knew she was trying to swallow her fear. It's scary to go against your instincts.

"Okay, so pull me in and, at the same time, drop to one knee and see what happens."

She tentatively did so, and I launched myself forward as if yanked, pretend-smashing my face into the wall above her.

"You're using his own momentum against him. You don't have to be stronger than him, you just have to *time it right*. That's the beauty of it. And he'll never expect it."

She nodded again, eyes determined, looking more certain this time.

"And check this out," I said. "In order to break my fall, I have to let go of you, see? And then you can run. Let's try again."

We went over it every day for a week, and on the second-to-last day of camp, I saw the exact moment when she *got it*, when she realized she had more power than she ever imagined, when she saw all the possibilities slapped into her hand like tickets at a carnival.

And I thought, this is what love is: all the possibilities.

My life wasn't perfect or anything before the diner.

But there were so many colors.

4

I WAKE UP SATURDAY AT ELEVEN, GROGGY AND OUT OF IT, to the sounds of the homecoming parade a few blocks over. The marching band is its usual loud, flute-heavy self. I haven't slept this late in years. Normally I'd be home from practice, showered, and on my second strawberry smoothie by now.

The brass and drum sections take over for a second, a fast, erratic, rat-a-tachycardia, and the band moves into the distance until it disappears completely. I try to stretch under the covers, but my leg muscles are killing me. At first I think it must be from sparring class yesterday, but that doesn't make sense because I didn't *go* to sparring class yesterday—*Oh.*

It's from crouching under the table at the diner, every fiber of my body tense and shaking.

There's a knock on my door, but I don't know why they bother because a second later, Hunter and Mom plow inside without waiting for me to say "Come in."

They're carrying trays of food. It's like a parody of hotel room service. Orange juice, pancakes, milk, yogurt, fresh fruit, and muesli. Usually these are my favorites, but today the juice hurts my eyes and the food looks nauseating.

"Dad's making omelets, too, but we weren't sure if you felt like coming downstairs yet," says Mom. "So whatever you want to do is fine."

"How'd you sleep?" Hunter asks.

I didn't dream, if that's what he means. Probably 'cause of the sedative. But being knocked out isn't the same as sleeping. It's not restful. It's just time you don't remember.

Hunter looks exhausted. We have similar features, but they came out wrong on me, like secondhand clothes. If his short curly hair is a buttery-golden sunflower, my straight thick tresses are the color of dandelions—nourished with acid rain. If his eyes are the clear aquamarine of a thirst-quenching mirage, mine are a dry, hazel-colored chalk and the boring sidewalk beneath it. He struts around the high school winking at people, but if I try to wink, people think I should get that tic checked out by a doctor.

“I thought you were supposed to be on the lacrosse float,” I say flatly.

“The other guys can do it. Do you want anything else to drink? We’ve got cranberry juice, too, I think, and grapefruit.”

Two sets of wide, hopeful eyes urge me to react, but I can’t muster a response.

It’s easy to see how Mom had a son like Hunter. They’re both bright and upbeat, a matched set of silverware in a catalog, and I’m the replacement knife thrown in at dinner because the other ones were in the dishwasher.

Mom is tall with a soft, round face and curly, chin-length hair, a wide mouth, and thin lips that never have to reach far for a smile. Everything about her is soft, from her faded flannel shirt with tiny beige buttons, tucked into her dark-wash jeans, to her rolled white socks and worn, creased loafers. She used to dye her hair, but now she lets it stay gray, and it’s even softer now, not loaded down with chemicals. Her nails are filed round, not painted talons like some kids’ moms’. Her softness is at a remove, though. There are no edges or solid surfaces to delineate her from her surroundings. When someone’s that soft, what do you hold on to?

At my belt tests, she used to gasp and wince and cover her eyes whenever I got thrown; it made Grandmaster Huan laugh. I know it’s because she loves me and didn’t want to see me hurt, but if she’d been watching, she would’ve seen how I always bounced back, that it was all part of the process. The fact that she didn't acknowledge my abilities hurt me worse than falling on my butt a hundred times.

Hunter could never do anything to make her cover her eyes. He wouldn't know how.

"Thanks, but . . . I'm not really hungry. Sorry." They probably ran to the store this morning, made a list, spent an hour cooking. I feel like a jerk.

"That's okay. That's fine, sweetie. We'll just set this here in case you change your mind," says Mom.

But they don't leave.

"I think I'm gonna go back to sleep," I mumble, pulling the covers up.

"Gretchen called," Hunter says, perching on the corner of my bed. I fight the urge to nudge him with my foot, make him move. Despite his cry fest last night and our temporary truce, we're not supposed to be speaking, and he's still not allowed in my room. "If you want to call her back, I can grab her number."

I don't respond, and they still don't leave.

"I'll call you on the intercom if I need anything," I add. We don't live in a fancy house, by the way; the intercom's for my dad, who's been in a wheelchair the past year.

"We'll be right downstairs," says Mom, pausing to stroke my face and kiss my forehead.

I try not to flinch.

I wonder if I should try to find him or something, my friend from under the table. We never got a chance to say anything to each other, and I'd like to talk to him, see if he's okay. See if he remembers things the way I do. But the cops split us up right away for questioning, to "independently corroborate our stories."

"It's just protocol," they said. "We want to hear separately from you both about what happened so we can fill out an accurate account."

I couldn't form sentences, though, so they didn't keep me long.

Hannah and DJ stop by around four o'clock, still in their band uniforms.

Mom spies them coming up the walk and asks if I want to see them. I tell her it's fine, and I open the door just before DJ rings the bell. It's warm for mid-September, and marching plus polyester has made them sweat. DJ's hair is stuck to her neck.

Hannah plays second-chair trumpet, and DJ is a baton twirler. They're my backup best friends, the understudies to Shelly Eppes, who ditched me for Hunter three weeks ago.

Shelly didn't "lose" her virginity to him; she threw it at him like a hand grenade. Not that he minded. I'm the one whose life exploded.

If she hadn't chosen him over me, I never would've been at the diner. Until recently, Shelly and I spent every Friday night at the gym, warming up for our respective classes: ballet for her, Tae Kwon Do for me. You wouldn't think dance and martial arts have much in common, but we were always finding ways they overlapped. I helped her with confidence and strength training, and she helped me with stretching exercises and flexibility. She taught me that you have to tear the muscle down before you can build it back up again. We were each other's secret weapons.

Hannah and DJ bubble over with gossip. We won the homecoming game, apparently, but that's not their big news.

"There was no kissage. Can you believe it?" Hannah asks.

I nod blankly. I have no idea what they're talking about.

"With Philip," DJ adds.

That's right, she and Philip had their first date last night, and Hannah tagged along. Deepti Ajarajollamon (hence the nickname DJ) comes from an old-school East Indian family that's forbidden her from dating without a chaperone. They asked me to go, too, but I opted out, and then I felt depressed warming up for class without Shelly. When Gretchen invited me to the diner, I grasped at her invite as if it were a life preserver. It was the first sparring class I've missed in years.

"We dropped off Hannah, and I'm—can we come in? Why are you in your pajamas? How come you weren't at the game?" DJ asks.

I realize I'm blocking them from getting in the door.

"Sorry. I think I'm coming down with something," I say. This is not a phrase I would ever, ever use. "So it's probably better if you go." I tap my fingers anxiously along the doorframe.

"Is that why you weren't there?"

"Uh-huh," I say.

"What's wrong? You look . . . kinda trashed," says Hannah, using one of her hands to flick her long blond hair behind her shoulders.

I look at my friends and I don't know them anymore. They're fresh and clean and normal, flushed from the day's activities, dressed in Abercrombie school colors. DJ's thick black hair has orange ribbons braided through it, and Hannah wears an orange headband to hold her bangs in place and frame her small forehead. They're always together. Hannah&DJ. DJ&Hannah. A gossiping, two-headed Abercrom-beast. It didn't bother me before, when I still had Shelly as my best friend and Hannah&DJ as the background, but now it does. I'm different from them, especially now; I'm set apart, and not in a good way.

"The diner was held up last night," I mumble.

They freak out simultaneously.

"Oh my God, Imogen. Oh my God. The diner where you were *at*?"

No, DJ, some random other diner in another state.

"Are you okay?" they sputter.

My mouth forms the words before I even think about it. "I didn't see anything," I say with a shrug. "I was in the bathroom. I called the cops on my cell phone."

The lie is so easy and smooth it feels true.

"Oh my God. You're like a hero," Hannah says.

"No big deal," I say, with another shrug. "I just gotta go lie down."

"Yeah, go, we'll call you later?" DJ says.

I make a mental note to turn off my cell. Forever.

"Yeah, talk to you later. Sorry I can't hang out."

"Oh my God, don't apologize," says Hannah.

"You have nothing to be sorry about," DJ adds. "Get some rest, okay?"

I know the lie I told them won't make me feel better. It's not even the lie I should have told. If I'd had time to formulate a better one, I would have. All I know is they can never find out the truth because they'll never be able to look at me the same way.

I wait till the middle of the night and then I sneak downstairs to Dad's office, my arms filled with belt certificates. Until I pulled them off my wall, I hadn't realized they were the only things up there.

It's not just belt certificates, though; it's awards: Best Attendance, Most Improved, Student of the Month, Best Tae Kwon

Do Spirit, and Best Demo Team Performance. I've gotten each of them at least three times.

The awards on my wall have defined me for so long there's never been room for anything else. With the exception of the pink-and-white-striped bedspread with lace trim and a teddy bear (wearing a black belt), my room doesn't even look like the room of a teenage girl. In the closet there's a secret poster of Hayden Christensen in *Jumper* that I used to kiss, but that's about it.

I'm able to get a lot of things through Dad's shredder before it starts making grinding noises. The problem is, there are so many things to destroy. Monthly schedules. Teaching sign-up sheets. Thick, dog-eared spiral notebooks filled with progress reports and diagrams of forms and techniques. Printouts. Binders.

How do you shred an entire life?

The next thing I know Mom's there in her robe, yelling and unplugging the machine and trying to pull my hands away from it. I want to elbow her in the solar plexus, but if I actually hurt her I don't think I'll ever forgive myself, so I just go limp and let her pull me away from the machine.

"Why are you doing this?" Mom cries. As usual, I'm incomprehensible to her.

She picks up one of the certificates I haven't shredded yet. She's got large bags under her eyes. The rest of her face is pale and pasty, and her hair is wild. "You worked so hard to get these."

"They didn't do any good," I whisper. *He died right there . . . so much blood . . . and I didn't do any good.*

I don't know why I'm whispering; I've obviously already woken her up. I guess I feel bad about it, 'cause she has to catch the train to work in a few hours, even though it's Sunday. She tries to hold me. She's soft and warm and smells like face moisturizer, comforting, but I don't close my eyes or sink into her embrace. I remain alert, poised to flee, my heartbeat a panicked stampede.

"It's okay," she murmurs. "Let it out."

Can't she tell I have nothing to give her?

Dad wheels in and turns on the light. The switches on the first floor have all been lowered so they're within his reach. The thought "Not my dad" slips into my mind like a drop of red dye in a bowl of water, staining it instantly.

When he showed up at the police station, I didn't recognize him because I was expecting someone six feet tall to come racing through the doors and scoop me into his arms. That was the vision I had in my head, sure to manifest any second, so I sat on the bench by the pay phone, next to the female officer who cut me out of my clothes, and I watched a stranger in a baseball cap roll up the ramp and through the automatic doors at the other end of the hall. I watched him disappear around the corner and wheel back in again, peering in doors, and the whole time I was thinking, *Where's my dad? I want my dad.*

"Go back to bed," I say.

"She broke the machine," Mom explains. "I'll pick up a new one Monday."

"What's going on?" asks Dad, his breathing labored.

I know I should feel guilty that I woke him up, too—guiltier, in fact, than I feel for waking Mom, because it takes a lot of effort for him to use the bars and hoist his plump body up into the wheelchair—but I don't feel much of anything because I'm still waiting for my real dad to come racing through the doors.

"Go back to bed, hon," he says gently to Mom, giving her hand a squeeze. "I'll talk to her."

I can't stop the mantra in my head; it comforts me with its rhythms and pacing, blocking out everything that's actually happening. *Not my dad. Not my dad. Not my dad.*

He removes his glasses and regards me. I think of football games and family hikes through the Old School Forest Preserve, of sitting on his shoulders as a kid, reaching up to brush the leaves of the branches above me as we went by, my legs dangling to and fro.

Not my dad.

"Imogen, no one expected you to . . ."

But it's easy to escape him.

All I have to do is walk upstairs.

5

ON THE LAST DAY OF SUMMER CAMP IN AUGUST, WE PUT on a talent show for the parents. Grandmaster Huan pretended to be a feeble old man with a cane. Ninja Cripple, we called him. When Chief Master Paulson attacked, Grandmaster Huan redirected the punch with his cane, whacked Paulson on the head, and then hooked the cane around the back of Paulson's knee and scooped it sideways so he fell spectacularly. The kids died laughing.

For my talent, I demonstrated breaking blocks of concrete with a hammer-fist punch (it's all about gravity and visualizing the impact beforehand), and then I showed how to throw a guy who's twice your size. After the first volunteer, none of the other dads raised their hands to be my next victim.

Taylor cheered the loudest. "That's my teacher!" she yelled to her mom. She told me she'd be signing up for the fall session, and she gave me a friendship bracelet she had made herself, embroidered with all the colors of the belts.

Shelly thought it was hysterical that the kids had to call me ma'am.

"It makes you sound like an old woman. What if you become a grandmaster?" she asked.

I giggled. "Then I'll be Grand Ma'am."

"Ma'ammary Master."

"Haus Frau Fu."

"Kung Fu is Japanese, not Korean," she pointed out.

"So?"

"So I thought you hated it when people confused the two. But fine. Spinster Sensei."

"That's Japanese, not Korean."

"That's what I just said!" she protested.

"Holy fuh, Shelly, you just totally insulted my style of martial arts." (That's the closest my friends and I come to "fuck." I don't remember which one of us started it.)

"Shut up." She laughed and pretended to kick me in the butt.

After the talent show, we drove across the border to Indiana, just because it was a starry night and we wanted to see it from someplace else. We zipped past the city, past Lake Michigan and the big Coca-Cola sign that writes itself in cursive, a letter at a time. We put one foot in each state and wondered where all the cornfields went.

We sat on the hood of Shelly's car and gazed up at the wide-open sky.

"Are we doing goals this year?" she asked.

"Definitely," I said, hopping down and grabbing some napkins and a pen from inside the car. "I'll type them up at home."

Every August, right before the first day of school, we made a checklist for the year and then held on to the other person's so we could mark off the goals once they came true.

"You start," she said.

"Okay. I want to hold a demo next week at school. Grandmaster Huan said if I get ten students to sign up for lessons, he'll give me six months free. And for the demo I get to choose the music, the routines, everything."

"Oooh, I'll make posters," Shelly said, which was awesome because she knew how to make them in 3-D, with several layers of letters popping out and intertwining with each other.

"Yay, thanks. What's your first goal?" I asked, pen poised.

"This year I'm quitting *Spectator*."

"Groan. You say that every year," I teased.

"I mean it this time. You have to come with me when I tell Mr. Andrews so I don't chicken out."

"I'll stand behind you and, like, glower in the background."

"Yes, be my enforcer! Wear your black belt."

"What are you gonna tell him?" I asked.

"The truth. I have to focus on dance if I want a scholarship."

"I'll totally come with you," I promised.

"Next goal," she said.

"Um, I want to get my license so I can drive myself to competitions. Next."

We went back and forth for a while until Shelly got quiet.

"I have an unrelated goal," she said, twirling a strand of hair between her fingers.

I was confused. "Unrelated?"

"Like, a personal life goal."

I rolled my eyes. "Homecoming?" Neither of us had ever cared about school dances before. "Are you turning into Hannah and DJ?"

"No." Shelly paused, looked down, and then looked back up. "Sex."

I was totally thrown. "What, just like zero to sixty? No kissing first?"

"Of course kissing. Not hooker sex! Jeez. Just . . . I want to have sex. That's one of my goals. I'm not saying it's going to happen this year; it's just a goal."

"Um, okay." I frowned but added it to her list.

There wasn't much to say after that. I probably should've asked if she had anyone in mind. I probably should have asked a million things, but I didn't.

On the drive home, I told her I wanted to open a martial arts school one day, and she told me she had an audition coming up for Manhattan Dance Company, Juniors Program. I figured everything was back to normal.

Monday morning. Three days since the diner. I wake up drenched in sweat, gasping for air.

I feel like a goblin came in the window while I was asleep and cut my chest open and replaced my heart. I just don't know what he replaced it with yet.

Whatever it is, *whoever's* it is, it's not mine. It's severely malformed; it's hard and tight and heavy, a compact nodule that spasms uncontrollably. There's a steel trap clamped around it, holding it in place so it can never escape. I can't tear it out, but I want it gone.

The phone rings at 6 a.m. It's Grandmaster Huan, calling from Korea, which is fourteen hours ahead. He's been there all month for his daughter's wedding. Mom answers and tells him I'm asleep, even though she sees me coming down the stairs when she says this.

“Why’d you tell him I was sleeping?” I ask after she hangs up.

She clears her throat. “He’ll be back in a week. You can talk to him in person then.”

She says I can stay home from school, and she stays home from work again, even though I tell her she doesn’t need to. Hunter brings me my homework, but I don’t even look at it.

Tuesday morning Hunter offers to drive me, but I’d rather walk. I forget to wear my coat, so Mom comes running out behind me.

On the way to school I see billboards for three different movies and a video game:

A woman in a bikini, holding a handgun behind her back

A man kicking down a door and firing a sawed-off shotgun

A man dropping out of a helicopter and aiming a machine gun

Two people pointing sniper rifles off a building

When I get to school, I have to pass the display case filled with sports trophies and team photos. Hunter’s photo is up there twice, MVP awards for baseball and lacrosse, his dimple on full display.

The last four issues of the *Glenview High Spectator* are also tacked up. One of them is about my Tae Kwon Do demonstration, which was last month but feels like a million years ago now. My picture's on the cover, an action shot. I've left the ground and I'm hovering in the air, my hair blown back dramatically, right leg extended, the exact instant the ball of my foot smashed through three boards. A BLACK BELT IN OUR MIDST! reads the headline.

I cringe, barely recognizing myself. The girl in the photo looks like she could handle anything.

The hallway fills up with faces of every color, all of us not-quite-Chicagoans living on the edge of the city. Glenview is somewhere between suburban and urban. Robberies and vandalism happen sometimes, but a shooting is still a rare event, and I hear people whispering about me—about what happened at the diner. I know it isn't paranoia. When I look at their faces, mashing and mawing, their mouths go into slo-mo and their lips form the words "Im-o-gen" and "Did you hear?"

When time returns to normal speed, Gretchen's there, her hand on my shoulder. Her hand feels firm and guiding, and I wonder what it'd be like to be one of her little sisters. *Better than being Hunter's sister.*

Her hair is curled and sprayed, her makeup impeccable. Did she spend all morning using her curling iron? That's either amazing or psycho. I haven't dragged a comb through my hair in days.

"I called you a hundred times this weekend," she says in a low voice. "Why didn't you call me back?"

I figured she just wanted an excuse to talk to Hunter, but right now it's obvious that's not true, and I feel stupid. "Sorry. I didn't call anyone back."

Every sentence I utter now begins with "Sorry."

"And why are you telling people you called the cops?" she says. "That's not what happened."

Dozens of eyes find me. The bell hasn't rung yet. I should have taken my time walking, should've waited till the last possible second before grabbing stuff from my locker.

"She hid under the table," Gretchen explains to the crowd. "It was really brave. I probably would've started screaming."

She actually thinks she's doing me a favor.

I close my eyes, utterly humiliated, and try to breathe.

A hand on my shoulder. Gretchen again. I open my eyes and let her blurred face come into focus. "Are you okay?" she asks.

Before I can answer, Hannah and DJ emerge from a different packed hallway, either coming to my rescue to lie on my behalf, without realizing they're lying, or to join the condemnation. Either way I don't want them to reach me. I turn my back and start digging all of my books and notebooks out of my locker, frantically gathering a pile in my arms.

The bell rings and the crowd breaks up. I turn around and bump into Hannah.

"What the fuh? Why'd you tell us you were in the bathroom?" she asks gently. Hannah's brow is wrinkled in confusion, and her eyes are moony and sympathetic, ready to pull the truth out of me. Or so she thinks. Some other kids hang back, their necks straining, waiting to hear my loser explanation.

How can I explain it was just easier? That if I'd told them anything but a lie they'd have said things I don't want to hear, that I can't hear, in soft, downy voices that would make me want to cry?

DJ hugs me. "We're just happy you're alive. But why didn't you tell us what really happened?"

"Because I didn't want to talk about it with you," I explode. "I just wanted you guys to leave, to stop breathing down my neck! And maybe because I didn't want to spend the next six hours analyzing why Philip didn't kiss you, okay? I had more important things on my mind."

DJ looks like I slapped her, and I feel stunned as well when I turn and walk away.

I didn't mean to say any of those things, and I don't understand how they poured out of me without my consent.

First period is a freebie.

Second period English is when it starts.

Grant Binetti takes the seat behind me and pokes me in the back, hard, in the shoulder blade.

When I turn around, he puts on an innocent expression like

he didn't do anything. I swallow and face front. He pokes me in the other shoulder blade, harder.

"Knock it off," I hiss.

"I'm just curious," he says to no one in particular. "What's the point of having a black belt if you don't do anything during a robbery?"

There are a few guffaws and a "Damn," and a bunch of murmurs as people consult one another. ("What's he talking about?" "You didn't hear?" etc.) Someone, I'll never know who, comes to my defense. "He had a gun, asshole."

"It's like one of those decoy cars," Grant continues. "You know, where they stick a cop car by the highway but there's no one inside? That's probably how Gretchen felt. She thought she was safe, having a black belt with her, but *she's* the one who had to call the cops."

I know why he's doing this. We all know why he's doing this. At my demo the first week of school, he heckled me from the audience, so I called him up onstage and let him make a fool of himself. Still, just because I know why he's doing it doesn't make his words any less true.

"You're right," I whisper. "I agree with you."

Grant's eyes narrow suspiciously and he has no retort, until after fifth period, when I discover a copy of the *Spectator* taped to my locker. In response to the headline A BLACK BELT IN OUR

MIDST! someone's written in the margins: "Liar," "Lame," and of course the catchall phrase, perfect for any occasion, "Bitch."

It hurts, but I don't know why; the words are laughably tame compared with what I've been thinking about myself for the past seventy-two hours. Doesn't Grant know there's nothing in the world he can write or say that will make me feel worse than I already do?

There were hints and warning signs long before this. I'm not a complete idiot; some of the stuff we learned from Grandmaster Huan was never going to be useful. It was taught only because it'd always been taught, because it was a challenging exercise, because it made sense in olden days, or because it looked cool, like Tiger Stance.

I might be small, but I'm athletic and toned. When I'm in the groove, spinning and kicking during class, I glow; I'm a power conductor, I'm electric impulses, I look like I really could beat the crap out of people. And maybe I *can*; but when we spar, we have to abide by certain rules. No hitting above the neck. No fighting before you hear "*Charyot*" ("ready position") and "*Joon-bi*" ("begin"). There's bowing and protective padding and tapping out so the other person knows to stop.

Real life doesn't have a whistle and *Charyot* and *Joon-bi* and bowing and protective padding and tapping out.

Why did I think it did?

....

When I get home from school, Mom and Dad have an update for me. The cashier's out of the hospital, recovering from surgery, and the gunman's funeral is scheduled for next week. It'll be a private ceremony—probably because of the condition of the body.

The cops don't need me to come back in, at least not yet, but they dropped off some info on counseling services. Mom also got a call from Principal Simmons, who told her they have a specialist coming in part-time from another district who I can talk to during school if I want. Mom thinks it's a good idea.

I sort of tune her out, though, because baseball play-offs are on and Dad's acting like himself again, hooking up the new TV (it's a tax write-off for him, since he writes about sports). He's sprawled on the floor like he's repairing a car—but he can't quite bend the right way to reach under the speakers.

I don't like watching him struggle like that, so I head to the kitchen for some water. When I get back, he's sitting on the couch, tray on his lap, eating a blueberry Toaster Strudel, complete with icing. Why do we even have those in the house?

While the national anthem plays, Dad draws a C for the Cubs on his Toaster Strudel with the icing, holding it up for me to see.

"One day," he says. "Just you wait."

"In my lifetime, hopefully," I add. I take the other Toaster

Strudel off his tray so he can't eat both of them, and I draw a Y for the Yankees on mine. I squish the tart until something pretending it was once a blueberry oozes out. Blue and white, perfect. With my nail I draw a slash over the Y.

"Excellent idea," says Dad. "Voodoo."

Doesn't matter who's playing the Yanks, we always root for the other guys.

We settle in for the game, our feet up, and I let myself relax. From my peripheral vision, Dad's wheelchair in the corner isn't so different from his easy chair, so for a moment everything feels familiar, the same as last year's play-offs, before he got diagnosed with diabetes.

But then he drops the remote and the batteries pop out, scattering under the couch.

I can't bear to watch him get down on the floor again and flounder around for them, so I dart down and pick them up and pop them smoothly back into place.

6

ON WEDNESDAY, WHEN THE BELL RINGS AFTER FOURTH period, I stay in my chair until everyone else leaves. Mr. Donovan, my statistics teacher (yes, I'm a junior in statistics, the training bra of math), looks at me over his glasses, eyebrows raised, but doesn't say anything.

Crowds in the hallway make me feel claustrophobic. I just need them to shift open a bit before I make my way out there.

I wait another couple minutes and then suck in some air and gather my nerves. I trudge through the hallway carefully, eyes down. I've become one of the slow movers who amble along without purpose. For the first time I can remember, there's absolutely nowhere I want to go.

I pass the water fountain and *there's me and Shelly, notebooks open, charts and diagrams, standing around like research assistants in a lab. Freshman year. She's writing an investigative report for the* Spectator, *rating each of the school water fountains. I'm helping her. I'm the control group.*

"Temperature?" she asks.

"Lukewarm."

"Tepid, would you say?"

"Yes."

"Taste?"

I make a sour expression. "Metallic."

"Height?"

"A bit high for me, and the arc of the spray always nails me in the nose."

"Convenience of location?"

"Eh. It's central, but there's always a line. The one outside the art room's a better bet."

"Breaking up" with Shelly was simple because we don't have any periods together except lunch. It was simple, but it wasn't easy. I see her constantly in my head, like the hallway's a portal to every time we walked it together and at any moment I might run into a different time-line version of us.

At lunch, I hide in the gym. I sit in the bleachers, all the way at the top, and pretend I'm watching my demo from a month ago.

It was the best day of my life.

It was everything this year was supposed to be: a series of

goals checked off one by one. The demo was first on my list, and I'd already made it come true. I'd assumed *all* my goals would come true. Now I don't even remember what they were.

There's comfort in reliving a day when I was completely in control of my actions, like maybe it'll provide clues on how to proceed from here.

I'm late arriving because there's a crowd at the gym door, and they all want to wish me luck; even a couple of my teachers are waiting to get in. The air is charged with excitement and anticipation.

I scan the bleachers for signs of obnoxiousness, threatened earlier by my friends, and see Hannah, DJ, and Shelly bobbing up and down, arms stretched high, doing a three-person wave. My face relaxes into a smile.

I gather my teammates, put my hand in the middle of the circle, and say, "Go Demo-licious!" It's silly, but they look nervous, so I want to make sure they have fun and don't freak out. I'm the oldest so I feel responsible for them.

Two whole minutes pass before the audience settles down and finds their seats. Looks like three hundred people showed up—that's ten percent of the school! When it's finally quiet and Principal Simmons walks over to the mic, Hunter cups his hands over his mouth and yells, "Go Imogen!"

Laughter fills the gym, centered on Hunter and his lacrosse friends in the first row, rippling out from them to the farthest corners of the gym. I laugh and cover my mouth.

"That's my sister!" Hunter yells, standing up, pointing at me and egging on the crowd. "She'll kick your butt! She'll destroy you!"

My teammates all laugh now, too, looking happy and less nervous. I don't even mind that Hunter's stealing attention from my moment. He can't help it. The spotlight's usually fixed firmly on him. Besides, he's probably responsible for half the audience being there.

Principal Simmons clears his throat and says, "All right, Hunter, thank you for your enthusiasm. With your permission, I'd like to start by introducing Glenview Martial Arts's very own demo team, led by Imogen Malley."

I tap the remote to my iPod and the Kill Bill sound track rips out of the loudspeaker. Since I organized the rehearsals and it's my "territory" (like I'm a drug lord or something), Grandmaster Huan thought I should get a chance to choose the music.

I call "Charyot! Joon-bi," and my teammates and I snap our arms to our sides and bow. Then Thomas and I move out of the line. He's just a freshman, but he's already a dark blue belt and knows the demo cold. Our sneakers screech loudly against the gym floor. At the dojang we always practice barefoot, but the high school won't allow it for sanitation reasons. Our uniforms look wrong with sneakers, a too-stark combo of ancient and modern.

Grandmaster Huan always makes guys the attackers and girls the defenders, because it looks awful to see men punching and kicking women and heaving them to the ground, but it's funny and awesome to see the opposite. And Grandmaster Huan wants to prove that his classes teach the weak to defeat the strong, no matter how unlikely it seems at first.

Thomas swoops at me with a left hook and I glide to the side, blocking his punch, grabbing his wrist, and yanking him forward, off-balance. I'm practically behind him now, and I feign a sharp kick to the back of his knee. I can feel the crowd lean forward in their seats, impressed.

The two yellow belts—I forget their names 'cause they were added at the last minute—demonstrate a simple front snap-kick block and a drop-sweep of the leg.

We exchange discreet high fives as they return to ready position. Their faces are flushed and exhilarated.

Even though everything's a blur, I try to slow time down and acknowledge the moment and remember exactly how it feels.

Thomas flies at me with a right straight punch and an immediate left. I redirect his fist using a crescent kick—echo-SMACK—spin around, and finish with a right ax kick to his shoulder. He recovers, gripping my shirt at the collar of my stiff cotton uniform, and I jab his armpit with my fingertips, which seems like nothing but is actually one of the most painful things I know how to do, then nail his side with a roundhouse kick and throw him to the floor.

The crowd gasps, then applauds, so I run a few maneuvers like my favorite block, where I do a cross-step hop and stamp on Thomas's foot, pinning him in place so I can pretend-bash him in the nose with the back of my fist. We never actually hit each other in the face, not even in sparring class. It's a rule.

"Should we do the flip at the end?" I ask him as he moves into a solid front stance and positions two boards high with both hands.

"Only if you break these," he says, adding a third to the stack.

I smirk. Triple-boards is supposed to look badass, but it's not any harder than one or two if you're used to it.

I take a few steps back, pause, and count to three. I close my eyes and visualize kicking all the way through the boards. I can do this. I open my eyes, right at the crescendo of the Kill Bill *music, and take a running start, springing into a jumping front snap-kick, and YES—all three boards are cracked in half, causing six pieces to fly through the air.*

Thomas looks alarmed for a second (he's supposed to hold on to them), but the fact that the force of my kick basically exploded *the boards is a plus in my mind.*

The crowd goes nuts, stamping and cheering!

Thomas catches my eye and gives me a nod. We'll be doing the flip. A totally unnecessary maneuver that nevertheless manages to make us look like superheroes. He bends at the knee and lowers his back so it's straight but parallel to the floor. I leap toward him, spinning in the air so my back rolls over his. I feel our vertebrae skid lightly across each other's as the world goes sideways, and then I land on the gym floor in perfect splits.

Standing O!!! The crowd leaps to their feet. They love us forever; they'll follow us off cliffs!!! I've never had so many people cheering for me before—I mean, people who matter. Not mall moms or kids at fairs.

My ponytail's come loose and strands of hair tickle my face. I brush the strands away and soak up everyone's adoration. My black belt test was comparatively low-key, with few witnesses. This *is what my black belt test should've been. A celebration. A crowd. Sweet acknowledgment from hundreds of my peers. I've earned this.*

Someone from the yearbook's filming me with a minicamera so I can show the demo to Grandmaster Huan later. He'll be happy with the size of the crowd and their response.

But then Grant Binetti shouts from the third row, "Who cares if you can break a bunch of boards? Anyone can do that!"

"Shut up, Grant. Why are you even here?" someone shouts back.

He doesn't answer right away, until more people chime in. "I'm just saying, it's not hard. Breaking a board doesn't mean anything."

What a massive tool! "Do you want to try?" I yell back, rolling my eyes. "Why don't you give it a try?"

"Yeah!" more people yell, pushing and shoving Grant out of his seat.

"Whatever." He nearly trips on his way down the bleacher aisle steps, onto the gym floor. He picks up a broken piece of wood. "These aren't even thick," he says. "They're like plywood."

I grab a fresh board from the unused stack and hold it out for him. "Here. Give it a shot."

Grant winds up and slams his fist into the board.

Nothing. Not even a crack. He's doing it completely wrong, and it's hilarious. He shakes his hand out, clearly in pain but pretending it doesn't hurt.

Grant tries again. And again.

Hollow. Thuds.

Principal Simmons rushes over to put a stop to it, looking stunned. He places a hand on Grant's shoulder.

"Okay, Grant, take your seat."

The crowd's laughing and taunting him now. "You're such an idiot." "Sit down, loser."

Grant glares at me, shoves the boards at me, and storms out the gym doors, letting them slam shut behind him. Whatever.

Principal Simmons grabs the mic again. "Okay, that's enough for today, I think. Thank you to . . ." He consults his note card. "Glenview Martial Arts for *that exciting show. The owner of Glenview Martial Arts, Grandmaster Huan, invites anyone who's interested to stop by his Tae Kwon Do studio for a free lesson and uniform." He consults another index card as I silently mouth along, "First month is only $24.95."*

I open my gym bag, pull out a colorful stack of promotional flyers, and hold them up so everyone can see, and then I set them down on a table near the exit.

In a wave, people tumble off the bleachers and crash to the gym floor, coming toward us. Toward me. *My friends can't even get to me. That's never happened before.*

I don't know who to look at. People swarm me; everyone wants to say something to me, to exist to me, to get a moment or a smile or a nod or a "Thank you for coming" from me. Handshakes, back pats, a few hugs from people I don't even know.

"Imogen! Hey, Imogen!"

"That was amazing*."*

"Oh my God. I had no idea."

"Can you believe Grant? He's such an ass."

"How long did it take to get your black belt?"

"Does it hurt to do splits?"

"How much did you have to practice?"

"When did you start taking lessons?"

"Are your dates scared of you?"

"What dates?" I almost say, but don't. That would be a dork's answer. So instead I just laugh in a manner that could be considered "knowingly," like "How right you are," but don't actually answer. They'll supply a witty comment

in their own heads. Because when you're suddenly popular, it doesn't matter what you're actually like. Everything you say and do is the most perfect thing to say and do in any given moment.

Is this what it feels like for Hunter after he leads his team to victory? It's addictive.

For a full week people stopped me to congratulate me, especially for what I did to Grant Binetti. He was always knocking into people—girls—in the hall, and last year he slammed his shoulder into Shelly, and she tripped and twisted her ankle. She had to sit out the spring dance recital—couldn't even be in the background—all because of him. It'd be like if I got demoted to *white belt* all of a sudden. I'd die of humiliation.

It wasn't just the best day of my life because of the crowd. It was the best day because of who was *in* the crowd. Shelly. Hannah. DJ. Hunter. All of us, friends.

And now, a month later, I'm not even sure who that girl was—that girl who stood up in front of her classmates and pretended to know how to fight.

I'm ripped out of my memories by the bell ringing. I haven't touched my lunch. I chuck it in the garbage on my way out the gym door.

The next couple nights I don't sleep. I just lie there staring at my now-empty walls, and then the sun comes up, and I realize I never drifted off, and now I have to go about my day, which is nothing more than a series of movements I make to fool people into leaving me alone. Mom has to come upstairs and drag me out of bed, as though I've slept, as though I've had some time off.

When I finally turn my cell back on, there's a text from Shelly, dated three days ago.

"Heard what happened. I'm here if U want 2 talk."

I should be relieved, but it feels wrong, somehow, to text back. Like it's unfair or against the rules to take advantage of this olive branch. If we're going to talk again, I want it to be because we're friends again, not because she pities me or feels obligated.

I read the text a million times until the words don't make sense, until they're just a bunch of unrelated letters and spaces that can't hurt me, and then I shut my phone off.

Friday night again. One week since the diner. One week since my heart transplant.

Hannah and DJ insist on taking me to the movies, as though I'd never snapped at them. Philip's coming, too. My parents think it's smart for me to get out of the house for a few hours and take my mind off things. Interesting that Mom didn't suggest I go to sparring; it's the second Friday in a row I've missed it. Does she know I can't possibly face anyone at Glenview Martial Arts? Is that why she wouldn't put me on the phone with Grandmaster Huan?

Hannah and I meet up at DJ's to help her get ready.

"Okay, this is how we'll play it," Hannah says, pacing around the room and slapping her hands together. "Imogen, you and I will get up *right* at the start of the last preview and act like we forgot to get a snack, and when we come back in, the theater'll be dark and we 'won't be able to find our seats'. . ."

"No, I don't want to be alone with Philip—the whole point is it's a casual group thing and not a real date," says DJ.

"That's just for your dad," Hannah says impatiently. "We don't *actually have to do it that way*. It just has to appear that way." She grins. "Do you want to get kissed or not?"

"Imo, hey, earth to Imo," DJ says, waving a manicured hand in my face.

"You okay?" says Hannah.

"Huh?"

"You've been spacing out. Philip's gonna be here any second, and we still haven't come up with a list of conversation topics."

"Are you sure you're up for this?" Hannah asks, sitting down next to me on the floor. "Do you want to stay in and rent something instead?"

DJ nods. "We could totally do that. Whatever you want."

They stare at me, all concerned, and I know if I said the

word, they really would stay in. They're better than backup best friends; they're the real deal.

"It's fine," I say, striving for a cheery voice. "But Hannah, you should ditch the skirt and wear jeans like me, so Deej will stand out more in her dress, and Philip will think she looks extra-feminine."

"Brilliant!" says Hannah, immediately grabbing her pants, slipping them on under her skirt, and then shucking off the skirt.

"You're a genius," says DJ.

I can do this. One word at a time. It's not too hard, really. Acting normal.

I spend the entire movie feeling trapped because I'm in a middle seat instead of an aisle seat. How psychotic is that? It's a romantic comedy, and people behind me laugh a lot, so it must be wacky fun. I don't remember anything about the plot.

Outside, I gasp in lungfuls of cool air and wipe sweat off my neck. DJ and Philip are holding hands so I guess Hannah's ploy worked.

Grant Binetti and one of his jerk friends exit the theater at the same time. He catches me looking and snaps, "What?"

"Leave her alone," says Hannah, pulling me along. "Loser," she mutters under her breath.

Grant and his friend walk off, dropping their ticket stubs on the ground. They were at *Legend of the Fist*, a martial arts flick—probably the same one I would've chosen before the diner.

My friends and I zip up our coats and turn on our cell phones. I'm the only one whose phone beeps, indicating a text. I have to pass Shelly's message en route to retrieving the text.

"Hunter's closing at Dairy Delight and wants us to stop by," I report.

"Free cones?" says Philip way too ecstatically.

Behind his back, DJ gives me the "please, please?" puppy-dog eyes. Even though I'm not really in the mood for Dairy Delight aka Dairy Dump aka Hunter's Harem, this is all part of being normal, and I find myself agreeing.

As soon as we get there I regret it, because the place is packed.

The horrible thing in my chest that's not my heart starts thumping like crazy and rising up my throat, too big to fit inside me.

All Hunter's friends are there, the who's who of Glenview High, including Gretchen and everyone from the diner. Worse, they're standing on tables and clapping for me.

IN SECONDS, I'M SURROUNDED. IT'S LIKE A NIGHTMARE version of my demo at school. That time, I lapped up every drop of attention and adoration. Now I wish I could fall through the floor.

"How are you doing?"

"Are you okay?"

"I can't believe it happened right after I left."

"It *sucks* you had to go through that."

Out of habit I scan the crowd for Shelly, poised and regal as an Abyssinian cat, but of course she's not here. She and Hunter didn't last, shock-o-rama.

"Hey, Imo," says Hunter. "How was the movie?"

He hands me my favorite dish: vanilla-strawberry sundae without nuts, sprinkles, or cherries because I hate crunching or chewing when I eat ice cream.

"Pretty good," I say, taking the dish. "Thanks." For a moment, I let myself chill. Hunter is the reason Shelly and I aren't friends anymore, but right now he's trying really hard; this is exactly the kind of party he'd want if something bad happened to him.

I wonder if this is what Oprah means by "eating your feelings," because Dairy Delight fare is the definition of comfort food for me. The store's been in Glenview forever, getting by on little kids' birthday parties, but these days it's actually popular with everyone at school, and not even in an ironic sense.

Hunter started working here a year ago, and his social life came with him. He's turned the place into a moneymaking machine, probably quadrupled the owners' income, and so no matter how much he (a) slacks off, (b) offers "samples" the size of regular cones, and (c) takes breaks every fifteen minutes to come out from behind the counter and dance with his buddies, he'll never be fired.

Everyone's so happy in his presence. The feeling's contagious, especially when he turns the radio up on a live concert going on in Grant Park and twirls me around in the middle of the store. I laugh despite myself and flick a dollop of strawberry sauce at him. It feels good to smirk, halfway to smiling.

A few minutes later, Gretchen pulls me into a hug. Even though she crushes my ribs, I hug back. She's cut and dyed her hair since I saw her last, and I tell her I like it.

She looks sheepish. "You do? I needed a change. It's so cliché, right? My trauma cut."

"Maybe I should cut mine, too," I ponder.

"But you have such beautiful braids."

"Oh, thanks."

Awkward City, population: two.

"How are you doing?" she asks finally.

I look down, rub the toe of my shoe against the black-and-white-checkered floor.

"She's still beating herself up over it," Hunter tells Gretchen.

"Why?" Gretchen says to me. "There's nothing you could have done."

I could have nailed him with a kick or a punch before he saw it coming. Damaged his kidneys. Smashed his balls. Taken out his legs.

I could've *tried.*

Effing "Daryl." I'd give my life for a fair fight with him. No weapons except ourselves.

"Thank God Gretchen was in the bathroom, huh?" says some dude I vaguely recognize from our table last Friday.

"If I'd been at the table, I couldn't have risked using my cell phone. He might have heard me," Gretchen adds.

Yet another difference between us. It never occurred to me to use my cell phone. Not even once.

"I would've hid under the table, too," Gretchen insists.

Which is all fine and good for *her*. She wasn't trained to do anything else.

"See?" says Hunter. "No one expected you to do anything."

Here's the thing, though.

Why not?

A while later, Gretchen finds me in the bathroom. I can see now her face is a bit blotchy and she's wearing lots of makeup under her eyes to hide the bags. I really wish I'd called her back last weekend.

"My parents put me on Xanax, like, twelve hours after it happened," she confides. "I can't concentrate on anything, but I have to focus if I want to win class president. I can't fuck up my whole senior year just 'cause of this." She reminds me of Shelly, all focus, focus, focus. I guess coming to school looking perfect is her way of dealing.

"They gave me a sedative," I admit. "It helped, I guess, but mostly it just made me feel groggy."

"You should definitely consider Xanax," she says, sounding like a pharmaceutical ad. "Ask your doctor." She reapplies her lipstick, then makes her way out the door to hand out pins and flyers to everyone. She's a shoo-in for prez; she'll get the sympathy vote *and* the hero vote.

She's spent a good portion of the night at my brother's side, but Hunter never returns to ground he's already fed from, and she's like eight girlfriends ago. Nearly every girl at the Dump tonight is an ex- or a pre-girlfriend. The Hunterettes.

"Stop looking at Hannah," I murmur at him when I emerge from the bathroom.

"What? Why?"

"You know why."

"First of all, I'm not looking at Hannah. And second of all, I think it'd be cool if you dated one of *my* friends. We could go on doubles." He takes a gulp of his frothy-looking purple soda. The only reason he has a job is so he can take out girls. He even gets paid in cash, so whatever he makes on Friday he can spend on Saturday without having to miss a beat and stop at the bank.

"I don't need you to pimp me out," I groan. We shouldn't be doing this here.

"It's not like that," he protests. "Jeez, go to a dark place much? I'll set you up with whoever. Someone nice."

"Forget it," I mumble, turning on my heel and marching toward the Love Experiment. "Deej, your dad's gonna flip his shit if you don't get home by eleven thirty."

My friends and I don't usually say words like *shit* out loud, but for some reason with the seniors standing around I feel compelled to pretend it's standard usage.

Hunter has to clean the place, restock the ice cream, and lock up, so it's pretty much time for everyone to go anyway.

We all head out the door, and Gretchen hugs me again. Just before she hops in her car, I realize she might be able to help me. I jog over and she rolls down her window.

"Hey, do you know who that other guy at the diner was?" I ask. "He was across from me, under a different table."

She thinks for a moment. "I didn't catch his name. I don't think he goes to Glenview."

I let out a breath I didn't realize I was holding.

Figures.

8

IN SECOND PERIOD ENGLISH LIT, OUR FALL READING AS-signment is *Bleak House* by Charles Dickens. Each fall the junior class has to read a Dickens. It's tradition, the notorious hell assignment of Glenview High, and is harder than whatever we'll have to read senior year, because by then the smart kids have been pulled into AP classes and the rest of us bumble along like always—by senior year teachers feel sorry for us and try to help us coast into college.

Guess which book Hunter got assigned when *he* was a junior?

Guess, guess, guess.

A Christmas Carol.

A CHRISTMAS CAROL! Which everyone already knows the

story of! So the day before the exam, he Netflixed the Disney version, where Scrooge McDuck is . . . wait for it . . . Scrooge. And Goofy is the ghost of Marley or whoever, with the chains. But my point is, SCREW THAT. Why should I have to read ten thousand pages about a house, when last year's juniors got to slack off with "God bless us, every one"?

Bleak House is so heavy that dirty cops could use it to beat confessions out of people. I want to fling it down an empty hallway and see how far it glides. Maybe after school, after the janitor's gone by with his whirring cleaner machine and the floor is all slick, I'll do just that.

Halfway through class, someone named Ricky Alvarez and I are called to Principal Simmons's office over the loudspeaker.

"Oooooooooh," says my English class, predictably. Mr. Andrews gives them a sharp look and they stop.

I take my backpack in case the bell rings while I'm gone.

"Try not to hide under any tables on the way," Grant calls after me.

Outside Principal Simmons's door I see a tall, built, dark-haired guy waiting. Must be Ricky. Probably a senior.

His sneakers are old and tattered. I don't know why I notice this. He's looking at the display case, where the damn *Spectator* newspaper article is, but when he sees me in the reflection, he turns around.

I don't meet his gaze, though, because I don't meet anyone's gaze these days.

"Don't you recognize me?" says Ricky after a moment.

Confused, I force myself to look up from the floor, up his legs and along his body, until I'm looking him in the eyes.

I hear gunshots, the cashier crying, and police sirens, but I don't look away.

He's my friend from under the table.

"Are you okay?" we ask each other in unison.

"I guess," he says.

"Not really," I go.

He sort of laughs and exhales and looks away for a second. "Yeah. Me neither. That was some fucked-up shit."

It doesn't sound obscene coming from his lips. It sounds accurate.

I'm acutely aware of my breathing, which has sped up.

"I was worried I made you up," I blurt out, which is probably the cheesiest thing he's ever heard.

But he just says, "I know. I kept wondering what happened to you. They couldn't separate us fast enough, right?"

"Yeah, I know." I'm nodding like crazy, so relieved we found each other. I jerk my chin toward Simmons's office. "D'you know what this is about?"

"I have a couple ideas."

Some acne scars dot his cheeks and forehead, but they just

make him more beautiful, because he's real, he's so wonderfully real, and he's the only one who'll ever understand. I'll be under that table, on some level, for the rest of my life, but so will he.

"Did you get any of your clothes back?" I ask.

He shakes his head. "They bagged it all for evidence. This is gonna sound dumb, but I was so pissed about my shoes. It's not like I'd be able to wear them, or even *want to* now, but they were—"

"Brand-new," I say.

He stares at me. "Yeah."

"I remember how white they were."

"Yeah. *Were*. I saved two months for those sneakers." He points to the dirty ones he's wearing now. "I had to get these back from the church rummage sale. I was planning on throwing them out, but my *abuelita*—my grandma—made me pack them up for the church, and then I ended up having to pay five dollars to get them back."

This is the longest conversation I've had with a boy who isn't Hunter or mandated by a teacher to talk to me because of a group project.

"Sucks," I say.

"No doubt." He pauses, lowers his voice. "You had it worse, though."

"I don't know . . ." I shrug him off. The thing inside my chest that's not my heart thuds to a halt, causing poison to back up into my bloodstream.

"I mean, it looked pretty bad," he says.

"No, yeah, I mean . . ." I cannot, *cannot* think about this.

There are gaps in my memory I don't wish to fill. *I'm under the table, looking into Ricky's eyes . . . and then there's blood everywhere, on me, on my clothes, on my face . . .* But there's something else first. *Under the table . . . Ricky's eyes . . . and blood. What happened before the blood? Why was I covered in it? What am I missing?* The school hallway twists into a funnel, and I suck in huge gulps of air, but it's not enough, not enough, not enough to clean me out . . .

"Sorry," he says quickly. "Sorry. You probably—"

The door opens and Mrs. Hamilton walks out. "Ricky, Imogen." She tilts her head, regarding me. "Are you okay?"

I nod. Her interruption has provided enough of a jolt that my train of thought has derailed. Oxygen floods my veins at last and I calm down.

"Thanks for waiting. If you'll follow me, please."

Mrs. Hamilton is the part-time school counselor, the one Mom mentioned to me. She must be the person who broadcast our invitation to this little reunion. At this moment I love Mrs. Hamilton.

"What's your name again?" Ricky asks, falling into step beside me.

"Imogen."

"Imagine?"

"No, uh, 'im' as in 'him,' and 'oh,' and 'gin.'"

He's quiet for a second, as if committing the pronunciation to memory. "Got it."

"Hunter's sister," I add, kind of rolling my eyes, because even though I hate it, it's the easiest way for people to place me.

"Don't know him," Ricky says, which makes me want to throw my arms around him. "Ricky," he adds, holding out his hand.

"I know," I say. "I heard it on the loudspeaker." And from Mrs. Hamilton.

"Right."

Mrs. Hamilton has us sit down in her office, which is covered in framed diplomas proving her qualifications to treat us. It reminds me of how my room used to look.

Her hair's cut in a bob and streaked with unapologetic gray stripes, which I totally respect. It reminds me of my mom's. Several wide, colorful bracelets on her wrists clank against each other when she moves her arms.

She explains that the school wants to offer us on-campus counseling for the rest of the semester during study hall. We can decide if we want to speak with her separately or together. It's up to us. I know which one I'd prefer.

"Water?" Mrs. Hamilton offers, moving toward the cooler in the hall.

"Sure," I say.

When she's out of earshot, Ricky and I immediately scoot our chairs closer.

"It's Monday," I sputter. "It took them *ten days* to decide we need counseling."

"More than a week!"

"I bet they formed a committee to decide if we were crazy enough."

"And a budget meeting to decide if they could afford it," Ricky adds, laughing.

"It's a good plan, because if it only takes a month for us to get over this, we'll know something's seriously wrong with us."

We're both howling now.

"What if we'd been totally fucked up already?" he cries. "We might have been off the deep end already."

I giggle. "Did they hope if they waited ten days we might forget what happened and not need counseling after all?"

Ricky snorts and wipes his eyes. We're basically in hysterics, but we force ourselves to curb it when Mrs. Hamilton returns, three paper cups in her hands. She looks at our chairs and how close we've moved them; perhaps she wonders if she should disapprove.

"What about Gretchen?" I ask, just to say something.

"Gretchen's parents were offered the same courtesy, but they've made other plans."

In other words, Gretchen's parents can afford a fancy private therapist. Suddenly, Mrs. Hamilton's cool gray hair seems haggard and her bracelets look cheap.

On the plus side, Ricky and I are getting along so well it's like I've known him my whole life. I'd like to think we would have found each other eventually, but maybe not. Maybe we needed the events of last Friday or we never would have met. He'd have graduated and left Glenview without knowing I existed. He doesn't even know Hunter! We could have lived here and gone to school and passed each other in the halls for months and never connected.

The other thing that's strange to think about is that if Friday hadn't happened we would both be completely different people right now, and maybe the person I used to be and the person Ricky used to be would have nothing to say to each other.

We decide on co-counseling, and Mrs. Hamilton excuses us, but we're obviously not racing to get back to class and she's obviously not racing to start "healing" us. She probably has to dust off her textbooks from the '70s and bone up on post-traumatic stress disorder first.

Outside her office, Ricky points to my *Spectator* photo in the display case. "Is this you?" he asks curiously, eyebrows raised.

My stomach tightens and I can't breathe. My imposter heart swells in my chest, threatening to rupture between my lungs.

Not him. Please not him.

"It's you," he answers himself. "Nice kick."

I can't breathe.

Anyone but him.

"Wait, you're a black belt?" he says. "Really?"

And then he laughs.

Both of us were laughing a few minutes ago; we were laughing our faces red, and it felt so good, but now he's laughing *at me*.

I punch Ricky so fast and so hard in the face that his nose bursts and he slams backward, cracking the display case right down the middle.

THE FIRST STUPID THING WAS THAT IT SHOULD'VE BEEN Daryl who got punched. The second stupid thing was getting into a fight right outside Principal Simmons's office.

Faculty members gather around just in time to witness me screaming at Ricky, "You didn't do anything either. You didn't do anything either." I have to say everything twice, because no one listens to me, no one hears me. I want to get down on the ground and pummel him, but not him—the gunman, the way I couldn't ten days ago.

Freaking Grant would have been a better target for my fist. So I guess there were two people I wanted to beat up, and Ricky wasn't even one of them, so how he got on the floor is kind of a mystery.

"Get up," I scream. He's not supposed to be on the floor, looking startled and bloody, broken capillaries spilling waste under his skin. My voice is hoarse. "Get up!"

"You broke my face," he moans, gingerly tracing his now-bulbous nose with his fingertips. Then he mutters, "Psycho bitch."

"Please get up," I beg, my hand trembling. I'm a black belt in Tae Kwon Do, but I've never punched anyone in the face. I've only mimed it all these years. We don't hit people in the face. Ever. "Get up, get up."

Principal Simmons calls my parents to come pick me up. I've been accused of "acting out," aggressive behavior, and damaging school property. But Mom's working and can't leave, and she took the minivan this morning 'cause she had to transport the flowers from Hunter's lacrosse float back to the nursery, and that means Dad can't get me either because he can't drive without the wheelchair lift. I'm a ward of the state or something.

"Spit it out," I say, when Simmons hems and haws over this unexpected snafu.

His face purples. "You listen to me, young lady. This is not a humorous situation. You are suspended until, until—Thursday."

You can tell he pulled that day out of his ass; it's totally meaningless. I don't know where I get the nerve to say, "What about my counseling sessions?"

"They'll be rescheduled," he says. "And, well, probably extended."

Get it? Because I'm CRAZY with a K.

"And they'll be conducted alone," he adds, which is when I finally realize how badly I've screwed up.

Despite the fact that I flat-out knuckle-blasted Ricky in the face, I thought maybe we'd still be in counseling together, helping each other through everything. My hand throbs, but to be honest I'm having trouble believing I punched him. It feels like I can still take it back, that he and I can still be friends. But of course not. I'm like a menace now. He'll probably get a restraining order against me, and I won't have anyone to *really* talk to about the diner ever again.

They want me off school property ASAP, so Hunter's summoned from gym class. He's in his dinky basketball shorts, complete with striped socks.

"What did you do?" he asks, pulling me by the wrist and leading me toward the front doors. I yank free, turning back to see Ricky staring at himself in the cracked glass of the display case, holding an ice pack against the bad meat that used to be his face.

Using my shoulder, I plow through the double doors.

"I punched Ricky Alvarez." The only one who might've been able to help me.

"Ricky Alvarez . . . Ricky . . ." Hunter mulls the name over and comes up blank. "Is he the guy who always orders root beer floats?"

"I don't know. Maybe you don't know him. He doesn't know *you*. Gasp, someone at this school has never heard of you. The mind boggles."

He lets my sarcasm slide. "Why'd you punch him?"

"I don't know."

"Did he try something with you?"

"No."

"Then what?"

"I don't know!"

"There must be a reason."

"He laughed at me, okay? I know I was useless during the robbery, but . . . I mean, *believe me*, I know."

"You protected yourself," Hunter says firmly. "That's nothing to be ashamed of."

How many times do I have to have this conversation? "You don't understand," I mutter.

"Why? Because I don't have honor or something?"

I don't reply.

"I wish I had been there with you," he says. "At the diner."

"Why? Because you would've stopped him?"

"No. So you wouldn't have been alone."

But I wasn't alone, I want to tell him. I'm only alone *now*.

We reach his car and I toss my backpack in but don't get inside. "I'll walk." I slam the door shut. Hunter tries to, like, manhandle me again. As if.

"I'm supposed to drive you straight home, and Dad's supposed to call the school and tell them you arrived."

"Let. Go." I shove his chest, hard, with both hands.

I know we're still on school property, and I'm probably being watched, but what does it matter at this point?

"What do you want me to do?" he cries, frustrated.

"Fight back," I reply.

"Go to sparring class if you want to fight someone."

"Sparring class isn't real!"

"I'm not gonna fight you," he says.

"You don't think I can knock you out?"

"I know you can; I'd rather not experience it, okay?" He rests his hands lightly on my shoulders. "What's gotten into you?"

I set off walking. He gets in the car and follows me, leaning out the window to try to talk.

"I know you hate me," he says, sounding tired. "I just don't know why."

"That's kind of the problem," I tell him. "That you don't know why."

"Is this about your birthday? Are you still mad about your birthday?"

Once upon a time I had a whole bunch of friends, until my brother picked them off one by one. Hunter's cupid doesn't bother with a bow and arrow, though. He sabotages the water supply and returns later to collect the bodies.

Whenever I had a group of girls over for pizza and a movie, Hunter would peek his head in the living room and tease everyone, asking what we were up to: "Gossiping about boys?"

I'd say, "Not you," hoping for once it would be true.

Next thing you knew, Hunter had a new girlfriend, and for a hideous month the Chosen One would show up at the house, no longer as my friend but as Hunter's toy, and breeze by me like she had more important people to see and I was the annoying kid sister in the way of The Relationship.

Within a few weeks Hunter would grow bored and dump her, except that didn't mean he'd actually dump her. That meant he'd stop calling her, and ask *me* to talk to her; so then she'd blame me or else try to use me as a reason to keep coming by the house and catch his interest again. This happened about eight times, no lie. By sophomore year, my real friends had been whittled down to precisely three.

Still, I just sort of accepted everyone's behavior until a month ago, my sixteenth birthday. The day after my demo at school.

A girl's sixteenth birthday is supposed to be special for two reasons—being kissed and being able to drive—but both were sore points with me: I was sweet sixteen and had never been kissed, and I was sixteen without a license or even a permit. Mom didn't have time to help me practice driving, or at least she didn't want to after work because it was too dark out and she got nervous about visibility, and I didn't really want to learn in the minivan with Dad, so I'd blown off the whole thing.

As for having "never been kissed," I'd dodged a feeble attempt during a triple date with Hannah and DJ over the summer. When Monsieur Tool leaned in, I totally gave him the cheek because we hadn't connected on any level the whole night; it was a pathetic joke that I'd all of a sudden want to *kiss him*. DJ and Hannah, of course, thought I was too picky; they figured you had to get it over with sometime, and if you waited for it to be perfect, it wouldn't happen at all, but I wasn't feeling it. DJ said that was *so* like a Virgo: too fussy and narrow-minded. (Yes, even my astrology sign has it out for me: Virgo, the virgin. Hunter's one year and one month older, which makes him a Leo, born lucky.)

So anyway, despite those two setbacks guaranteeing I'd die alone, I decided to throw a slumber party for my birthday, as a retro throwback and a way to kick-start the new school year. We talked about it all week. Should we do makeovers? Watch

DVDs from the '00s? Play "Light as a feather, stiff as a board"? Truth or dare? Paint our nails, braid our hair, and read horoscopes all night?

I told Hunter to make himself scarce, but he said he'd already requested the night off from work, and Mom and Dad said they needed his help cleaning the basement and setting up streamers and stuff. As long as he was there in a service capacity *only*, I decided it was okay. Fatal mistake.

Around midnight, Shelly Eppes headed upstairs to get my camera from my bedroom. I made note of this but forgot, because Hannah and I found the old sprinkler system, and she and DJ and I were having a blast running through it like we were kids again. The moon was bright, and it was still warm out, and we were being profoundly screechy, to the annoyance of the Mastersons, our next-door neighbors.

Later I realized Hunter wouldn't have missed the chance for wet T-shirts in a million years—unless he'd been in the midst of something better. I went inside and upstairs to grab towels and find my camera. Hunter's door was partially open and there were noises coming from his bedroom. I rolled my eyes and went to investigate, nudging the door all the way open. Shelly and Hunter were having sex, Hunter's naked butt bobbing up and down.

Shelly's thin, coltish, dancer legs were under his, but I didn't see her face. I sputtered in horror and slammed the door shut.

I wouldn't call it a deflowering. More like a weed whacking.

After being blinded by the image of Shelly and Hunter going at it, I sat in the kitchen, dazed and vomit-y, still in my damp shirt, thinking about every girl who'd ever used me to get closer to him.

Maybe I shouldn't have been as shocked as I was. *It was on her list of goals.*

Hannah and DJ asked me what was going on, and I filled them in, my voice shaking with rage and disbelief. Snapshot of Imogen at sixteen: unkissed, no license, no best friend.

A minute later the Happy Couple appeared, looking disheveled. Hunter gave me a sheepish grin, like "Whaddaya know?"

Shelly kept her face down, but her spine was perfectly straight, imperious, a dancer's posture as always. I stood in front of her and made her look at me. "Get out of my house," I told her.

"Whoa, calm down," said Hunter.

"Shut up," I growled at him.

"What about all my stuff?" asked Shelly, blinking too much, her face scrunched and red. She looked delicate, small, and confused. How dare she be confused! I wanted to shove her. I wanted to sob.

"How am I supposed to get home?" she said. "It's one a.m. What am I supposed to tell my parents? The front door's locked . . ."

"You know what?" I said. "I don't care. Just leave!"

"I'll drive you," said Hunter.

"I'll walk," said Shelly, not looking at him, as if that would help her cause, prove something to me, make everything okay.

"Fine," I said.

"Fine," she said.

Tears shimmered in my eyes. "And don't expect him to call you," I yelled to her retreating figure.

I was too angry to speak to Hunter. Hannah, however, was the right amount of fury and calm.

"I can't believe I used to wish you were my older brother." (Hannah's an only child.) "What a laugh." And she actually laughed then, this horrible, awesome, joyless laugh. "I can't believe I used to think you were cool. You are the *worst*, most selfish older brother a little sister could ever have."

Hunter's face transformed. The half smile he'd been sporting slid down his face, all the way off, and the bright color of his eyes dimmed, turning a murky-pond-water shade like mine. For a moment I swear all the blue went out, like something vital had left and wasn't coming back.

I didn't tell my parents I'd caught Hunter and Shelly doing it. I wanted something to hold over his head, in case I ever had a secret I needed him to keep from Mom and Dad.

But Hunter and I don't hang out anymore. We don't make fun of teachers or watch *Amazing Race* and strategize how we'd beat the other teams if we were picked for the show. He's not allowed in my room or at my Tae Kwon Do tests. We're just two people who have to live in the same house, and one of us hates the other.

As for Shelly, she made her choice. Part of me believes our friendship was never important to her, and part of me knows that's ridiculous. All of me hurts.

Funny how I thought *that* was going to be the worst thing to happen to me this year.

At home, Dad checks out my hand, squints at it, and declares it okay. Mom's not home yet, so we just watch tennis in the living room for an hour while Dad takes notes. He writes nonfiction books about sports, and his latest one details the history of the different kinds of tennis courts.

On-screen, the tennis ball is hypnotizing, and I try to turn my mind off, but I keep thinking about the punch. For a second, just one tiny second, without smiling or any other indication I might be doing this, I allow myself to be proud.

It was a really good punch.

The problem, and it's a huge problem, was that I didn't use it in self-defense. I attacked someone. Smashing Ricky's face like that went against everything I've been taught and everything I'm supposed to stand for.

There are five tenets of Tae Kwon Do:

Courtesy, Sir!

Integrity, Sir!

Self-control, Sir!

Wisdom, Sir!

Indomitable Spirit, Sir!

How could I toss them aside so easily? Especially self-control and integrity. If all the tenets are meaningless, just things I said in class so I could get my next belt, why did I bother? I've only been away from training for a week and a half. How did I lose my way so quickly?

Then again, maybe it's normal to want to use my training in real life, outside the walls of the *dojang*. Otherwise, it's like having a skill you never use, a present you never get to open. Total mind game.

Grandmaster Huan left another message on the machine this morning, saying he's back from Korea. Knowing he's teaching classes right this minute, right down the street, makes me feel anxious and unsettled.

Hunter's supposed to go back to school after "dropping me off," but even though I walked the whole way and it took half an hour to get home, he lingers in the kitchen, eating an apple and waiting to see if Dad'll give me a lecture.

Negative.

Shortly after Hunter takes off, Mom shows up and we all traipse into the kitchen for a Serious Talk.

"We want to make it very clear we didn't expect you to do *anything* at the diner last week" is Mom's opening gambit. "It would have been dangerous to interfere. Martial arts is great; it's a great sport—"

"It's not a sport; it's self-defense," I grit out.

"And it's great for that, I know, but it's not always about 'real life' incidents; no one expected you to stop what was happening."

"That makes it worse! You're basically saying everyone's been humoring me this whole time. 'How cute about Imogen and her little hobby. It's so adorable she thinks she knows how to punch and kick.' It wasn't sticker collecting!"

"That's not—of course not; that's not what I mean," Mom says, rubbing her forehead with the back of her hand. "It's so many things. It's good exercise; good for your health, your confidence, your self-esteem; a terrific way to meet people, be a part of something."

"How would you know? You could barely stand to watch my tests. You don't even know what I can do!"

"I know I'm not saying the right things—"

"I can't believe you knew this whole time it was a joke, and you didn't tell me. Why did you let me keep going? Why did you let me think it was real?"

She reaches for my hand, but I dodge her.

"It *is* real, but he had a gun, Imogen—"

"So then I must just not be very good at it. Is that what you're saying?"

"No, of course not—"

"You're amazing at it," Dad bellows out of nowhere. "You're the top student. How many kids have you taught? And I can't believe you're apologizing for protecting yourself."

I'm startled. For a second he seems six feet tall again, like he could pick me up and place me on his shoulders.

After a moment, Mom starts over. Her new opening line is, "We know you're upset."

They know nothing.

"But we do not get in fights," says Dad.

Mom is nodding like this is normal. "It's okay to scream and shout and have a good cry, but we don't hit people. Not in this family. Hit the punching bag in the garage instead. That's what it's there for. Right?"

They don't get it. The punching bag won't hit back.

"I forget sometimes that you're only sixteen," Mom says. She glances at Dad. "Which is why your father and I are deciding what happens next. No ifs, ands, or buts. You're going to go to this boy's house and apologize to him. And, to show him you're serious, you're going to bring him something you've spent some time and effort making. Okay?"

"Oh my God," I say, covering my face with my hands. Because I know where this is going. She doesn't mean a card. She means I have to bake cookies for him. BAKE COOKIES FOR HIM.

Ricky will probably take them to school and pass them around in horror. *Look what I got. Think they're poisoned? Filled with gravel? Who wants to try one?*

No one will be able to keep up with the narrative of my crappy, ever-changing identity. The Nobody, Hunter's Sister, the Black Belt, the Coward, the Liar, the INSANE COOKIE BAKER. How much longer will this go on?

I picture myself in various outfits, like Halloween costumes. A gorilla. A Native American Indian. A princess.

A martial artist.

Was that all it was, in the end? Nothing more than a costume I tried on?

We decide chocolate-chip is best.

10

AFTER CONSULTING THE SCHOOL DIRECTORY, MOM DRIVES me to Ricky's house at four o'clock, thinking he'll be home from school by then. Mom would normally be at the Congress Plaza Hotel in Chicago right now, where she works as a concierge, but my suspension has screwed up her schedule. I feel guilty she's skipping work because of me.

Ricky lives in a kind of not-okay part of town. All the cars parked on the street have the Club on their steering wheels, and shoved under the windshield wipers are flyers for massage parlors, accent elimination, and "Ladies Only!" specials at nightclubs and bars.

His apartment building looks scuffed and crumbling on

the outside, but inside the apartment it's actually really nice. Framed photos compete for space on the walls, like overlapping teeth in a smiling kid's mouth. There's Ricky, his older sister, his parents, and his grandma everywhere you look.

His dad's a marine, pretty ripped for an old guy, with medals and everything. I bet Ricky's dad puts a value on being healthy and fit and knows how to lift weights and run and swim and fight. I bet he knows self-defense, a military version of martial arts. Ricky's dad would understand what it's like for people like me. He would understand what I'm going through.

The smell of warm tortillas wafts over from the stove. I don't want to be here, but I don't want to leave either.

Ricky's nowhere to be found, so we have to explain everything to his ancient *abuelita*. She's the one who made Ricky donate his shoes to the church rummage sale and then buy them back. She doesn't seem surprised when we introduce ourselves.

"Terrible thing, last week," she says, pulling out kitchen chairs for us. "Terrible to see. Very upsetting. Ricky is very upset."

"Where is Ricky?" Mom asks.

"Playing basketball at the Y." She glances at the clock above the stove. "He won't be home until dinner."

I nod, handing her the tin of cookies. I can't decide if I'm relieved or upset. I'd dreaded the visit, but I'd also wanted an excuse to see Ricky again, even if he hates me.

I like sitting with his grandma, one degree away from Ricky; she seems like someone else who understands, and I don't want her to kick us out or look at me with disappointment.

"I did something bad," I say softly.

I don't want to narrow it down. If I just let that statement hang there, maybe it can apply to everything, starting at the diner until now, and I can be forgiven for all of it.

But I keep talking, shrinking down my apology until it forms an outline around the shape of my fist slamming into Ricky's face. After listening to the rambling story of how I knocked her grandson into the display case, Ricky's *abuelita* opens her mouth and laughs.

"He told me he was elbowed in the face in a game of basketball."

"Well, he wasn't," I say irritably. "It was me." Credit where it's due, yo.

She leans in, her eyes mischievous. "Did he deserve it?"

"No," I say, freshly ashamed, and not because Mom is staring at me like, "THIS IS SUPPOSED TO BE AN APOLOGY."

"Ahh, chiquita, he doesn't want anyone to know. It was black and blue all over." She gestures around her nose.

Huh! She's amused, not angry. She opens the tin of cookies and lifts it to her face, brushing the wax paper to the side so it won't tickle her nose. She closes her eyes, inhales, and smiles like a sleepy cat. "Mmm." She plucks a cookie from the tin.

"The sun, the moon, and the stars," she says, referring to the different cookie shapes.

Chocolate-chip cookies sound boring, but the way we make them is a bit different. One time when I was little, Mom ran out of chocolate chips and added a handful of butterscotch pieces in their place, so some of the cookies had a different flavor to them. Hunter and I thought it was deliberate (and we used to fight over who would get the butterscotch ones), so from then on we begged her to make them that way every time. Also, we don't spoon the batter onto the tray in individual blobs so they all turn out the same circle shape. It takes too long and "you may as well use premade Tollhouse for that," as Mom would say; instead, we scrape all the batter straight from the mixing bowl onto the sheet and spread it around from edge to edge. When they're done baking, we cut them into bars, make four gigantor cookies, or use Christmas cookie cutters. Maybe it's silly, but that's how we do it. Sharing this with Ricky's family is kind of like showing them who we are.

Ricky's *abuelita* offers us coffee and a cookie, but I check twice with her before I take one, since they're supposed to be a gift.

"What are you cooking?" asks Mom. "It smells delicious."

Ricky's *abuelita* gets up and ambles to the stove to lift the lid, releasing a heavy fog of peppers and heat and melted cheese. While they're distracted, I take the opportunity to look around the room. Propped against the wall are campaign signs, the kind people stab into lawns. ALVAREZ FOR CONGRESS is written on them in red, white, and blue, alongside a picture of a woman who must be Ricky's mom.

I recognize Ricky's backpack in the corner. A thick spiral-bound notebook pokes out of it. My mom and his grandma are chatting away at the stove with their backs turned, oblivious, so I quickly pick up the notebook and flip it open.

It's not a notebook, though: it's a sketchbook, with heavy off-white paper, and there are a bunch of charcoal drawings inside.

Some pictures are of me.

They're of my eyes.

11

THE NEXT AFTERNOON, TUESDAY, IS THE FUNERAL.

It occurs to me that the reason it's a private ceremony isn't because of the condition of the body but because they're afraid no one will come.

I feel sick picturing an empty church parking lot, but Mom and Dad refuse to drive me over to pay my respects. They don't want me to "wallow in guilt" for something that "isn't my fault."

Their words mean nothing.

I'm still grounded for punching Ricky, but I *am* allowed to walk to White Hen Pantry to pick up milk.

Shelly and I used to ride our bikes here every Saturday when we were in junior high. We sat in the magazine aisle and read as many tabloids as we could before the owner told us it wasn't a library. We liked quoting to each other from *Bop* and *Tiger Beat* and getting ideas for our own fake magazine, which we launched the following year to a readership of three. (Shelly's mom was in that phase of wanting to be our pal, so when she discovered a copy of the latest issue, she didn't chastise us for drawing a pinup of Mr. Levin in a Speedo; she just corrected our grammar and handed the pages back to us.)

Today when I'm here, I buy the milk and a newspaper and sit outside by the curb, reading the police blotter. I already knew the gunman's name (Daryl), but now I find out the cashier's: Lauren. Ages twenty-eight and twenty-two, respectively.

"What the hell are you doing, Daryl?"

"Just empty the register! Shut up."

Ricky and I aren't mentioned by name because we're minors. We're just described as witnesses, which makes us sound passive, like we watched everything unfold on a screen hanging on the diner wall.

Gretchen is mentioned by name because she's eighteen. They refer to her as "the resourceful teen who called 911."

The way the article is written, everything seems off. Some of the facts are there, but not all of them, as if the article is describing the shadow something has made and not the thing itself.

"What the hell are you doing, Daryl?"

"Just empty the register! Shut up."

It always bothered me that she knew his name. Why did she know his name?

When I get home, Grandmaster Huan is in our living room wearing a suit and tie. I've never seen him in anything other than his crisp cotton Tae Kwon Do uniform. He sits stiffly on the couch, his back a perfect straight line, like a bamboo stick is bracing it that way under his suit. It reminds me of Shelly and her dancer's posture.

Dad's in his chair, and he catches my eye when I pause on the threshold.

"Imogen," says Mom in her new voice, the high, tinny one that originated at the police station and is supposed to be cheerful but sounds vaguely insane, "Grandmaster Huan would like to speak with you." She stands and motions for me to take her seat.

I hand her the milk and she goes to put it away. I snap my hands to my sides and bow low to Grandmaster Huan. He nods curtly.

Not good.

Rules of conduct at Glenview Martial Arts, mostly for the twelve-and-under kids, are pretty strict and extend to home life. We have to be respectful of parents and siblings, keep our rooms neat and clean, and always do our homework and keep our grades up, or we can be held back on test day. Parents love it because they don't have to create incentives; they can just say, "I'm going to mark down for Grandmaster Huan that you didn't eat your vegetables."

And how dorky is this? I *loved* the rules when I was that age. They made me feel secure, like I was a martial artist 24-7 and that everything I did was important, because it reflected on Grandmaster Huan and his Tae Kwon Do studio. If I saw shopping carts scattered around the parking lot at Jewel-Osco, I'd organize them. If I saw garbage in the movie theater, I'd pick it up and throw it away. My room was spotless. My grades were as good as I could make them (usually Bs and Cs, but for me that took effort), and I never ate junk food.

So I'm pretty sure I know why Grandmaster Huan is here, and it makes me ill. His English is excellent, but his accent sometimes makes it hard to tell what he's saying. I don't understand every word today, not even close, but I don't need to.

"This is serious matter," says Grandmaster Huan. "I hear you hit another student at school. Is this correct?"

I stare at the living room carpet.

Mom returns from the kitchen and gently touches my back, but I shake her off and slowly raise my eyes to Grandmaster Huan's. "Yes, sir."

"This is not black belt behavior. What will smaller kids think when they hear you've been in fight?"

I think of Taylor, my sixth-grade student from camp, and my stomach hurts, like a bunch of golf balls are grinding against one another in my intestines.

"Mr. Huan," says Dad (major faux pas—he's a Grandmaster, not a Mr.), "there are outside circumstances, of which you are aware. Imogen saw someone killed right in front of her. She's been under a lot of stress and pain, and she's already made amends with the student she hit."

This isn't entirely true, because Ricky wasn't there yesterday, but I'm not going to say anything.

Grandmaster Huan nods again. "Yes, I am sorry. Yes, very sorry." He waits and thinks, and thinks and waits. "This is big problem. Very tough situation."

I don't know if he means for him or for me.

"Six month is standard. But this is different. I think you can come back January first," he murmurs.

"Three months?" I blurt out.

He gives me a pointed look. "This is not the first time you are in trouble," Grandmaster Huan says.

"What?" Mom cries.

"I've *never* hit anyone before," I say, confused.

"This is not the first time we have discussion about proper Tae Kwon Do spirit," Grandmaster Huan explains.

"Are you talking about the demo?" I ask. He'd pulled me into his office after he watched the footage last month. I figured he wanted to praise me; I'd gotten him fifteen new students, earning myself half a year of free lessons, but he didn't even mention that.

"This is not what I teach you," he'd said, frown lines all over his face. His computer screen was paused on Grant and Grant's futile attempt to break the boards. "Tae Kwon Do is not show-off."

I couldn't believe he didn't understand how annoying Grant was. "That guy was a jerk," I'd protested. "A bully. Sir."

"This is not what I teach you," he repeats today.

"But—"

"What is first belt color?"

"White," I mutter.

"What does white belt mean?"

"White belt signifies purity. No knowledge of martial arts," I say by rote. "No room for pride, ego, or conceit."

No room for the real world, I want to add. No room for guns.

I can't decide if martial arts failed me or if I failed it. Probably the second one. It never claimed to keep me safe from bullets, but I made vows I couldn't keep.

"I will improve myself mentally and physically, sir!

"I will respect my elders and teachers, sir!

"I will always defend the weak, sir!

"I will prevent unnecessary fights, sir!

"I will be a champion of freedom and justice, sir!"

So the decision's been made, and it's final. I'm stripped of my rank until January 1. Grandmaster Huan asks me to return my ID card, the one from the home office in Korea, and my belt certificate signifying first degree. It was the only one I didn't shred, maybe because it was my secret way of keeping them all, since they all led up to it.

In return, he hands me the framed photo of me in my black belt uniform, the one they had professionally taken on the day of my test. Until recently, it was hanging on the wall of the *dojang*, the only one of its kind.

"January first," he says, "We'll put this back up. Be good, prove yourself, no bad behavior until then."

Mom takes the framed photo from him. She knows it's not safe with me.

I rise on wobbly legs and bow to Grandmaster Huan. His eyes look sad. It can't feel good for him, kicking out his only teenage black belt. He bows back, just a flinch at the waist, and he also shakes my hand, which doesn't happen very often. When you shake a hand in your TKD uniform, you're supposed to use your other hand to press your sleeve flat against your arm, to show that you're not concealing any weapons. Grandmaster Huan does this now, out of habit, even though he's in a suit and tie.

He walks out the door, his back hunched and defeated, not straight like it was before.

Silence settles onto our house like a fumigation tent. We all just wait quietly to choke and die.

Dad clears his throat and says, "January first isn't too far away."

"Please don't," I say.

"Imogen . . . ," Mom says in warning.

"He's a *grandmaster*, by the way, his name is *Grandmaster Huan*."

"I'm sorry," Dad says. "I didn't remember—"

Before he can finish, I'm halfway out the room.

"Imogen," Mom calls after me.

I dart upstairs to the bathroom, lock the door behind me, and turn on the shower.

The urge to purify is overwhelming.

I yank off my clothes and stand under harsh, burning water and *I'm back at the police station, standing in the locker-room shower, nervous about my nudity, a thin plastic curtain separating me from the female cop, who sits outside to make sure I'm okay. She cleared the place out so I could have privacy, and she's got a towel, sweatpants, and a T-shirt waiting for me on the bench next to her.*

I will never get my regular clothes back. They are not clothes. They are evidence.

At the diner, the blood was sticky and weighed me down; I wanted to slither out of the blood and my clothes, *rip all my hair out* so I'd never feel that slimy again, but they wouldn't let me. They had to cover the inside of the squad car with plastic wrap, and we had to ride to the station that way, and then another twenty minutes passed before they cut me out of my clothes and let me shower.

When I dunked my head under the water, it felt like blood pouring over me, and I was afraid if I opened my eyes and looked down at my skin, it would still be coated red.

Low to the ground is comforting; standing up is bad.

Low to the ground is comforting; standing up is bad.

After scrubbing as hard as I could with the soap, I squatted in the shower, nice and low to the ground, right by the gross drain, and let the water smack down on me from a distance, hitting just the top of my head and my back in a *splat-splat* rhythm until the female cop said, "You okay in there?"

Today, eleven days later, I slide down the wall of my own shower and curl up in a ball, tuck my knees under my chin, and wrap my arms around my head. I've taken showers since the diner, but this one's different.

Get smaller. Small as you can be.

Low to the ground is comforting; standing up is bad.

Why is standing up bad?

What happens if you stand up?

(You don't want to know.)

Reset button. Start at the beginning.

Gretchen's in the bathroom when the gunman comes in.

I see the glint of his gun, and I hide under the table.

There's Ricky, under a different table; he brings his finger to his lips. Shh . . .

It's hard to breathe; my nose doesn't get enough air, so I open my mouth to inhale and exhale, in-out, in-out, in-in-in. The water droplets from the showerhead catch the light on their way down, and little portions of them disappear, but you know they're still there.

I'm starting to full-blown hyperventilate when there's a pounding on the bathroom door. Hunter. "Hey, Imo, how long are you going to be? I have to shower before my date."

"Gimme a sec," I gasp out. *Deep breaths.* I slowly unfurl, not quite standing, just high enough to turn off the water. Then I wrap myself in a towel and sink back down to the floor.

Low to the ground is comforting; standing up is bad.

I don't know how much time passes before Hunter knocks again. "Seriously, I need to use the shower."

I don't want to get up. I want to crawl out of here on my hands and knees. I pull my clothes back on and scoot out into the hallway on my butt. Hunter flies past me into the bathroom and closes the door behind him.

It's only seven o'clock, but I get into bed and pull the sheets and blankets up to my chin. There's no reason to stay awake; there's nothing I want to do except not be conscious anymore.

Mom comes in to check on me.

She presses a palm to my forehead. "Are you okay? Do you feel sick?"

I'm probably artificially warm from the shower. "No, just tired."

"Well, when you come down for dinner, I'd like you to apologize to your father."

"For what?" I ask softly, confused.

"For leaving the room before he's finished talking. It's become a habit of yours, and it's rude. You just get up and leave, without waiting to see if he's done. Okay? He's in his office."

When she leaves, I press the intercom button for broadcast and apologize to Dad. That way Mom will be a witness, too, but I won't have to go anywhere.

I wish I could say I bawled my eyes out over Grandmaster Huan's decision to kick me out. I wish I could say it gutted me and I couldn't imagine my life without martial arts.

But the truth is, I never had any intention of going back.

12

ON WEDNESDAY MORNING, THE LAST DAY OF MY SUSPENSION, Hannah stops by before school.

Minus DJ.

Mom says we can visit for five minutes, but that's it.

"I can't stay long anyway," Hannah says, shucking off her boots but not her coat. "So, what's it like being suspended?"

"Where's DJ?" I ask.

Hannah hesitates and then resets the barrette in her strawberry-blond hair. "She's kind of not allowed to hang out with us for a while."

"'Us'? You mean me."

"Because of the whole fighting-at-school thing."

Ah. I'm a bona fide bad influence. I can't really blame the Ajarajollamons, but it's still a bit of a shock.

Hannah and I make the most of our five minutes by frantically looking up Ricky Alvarez in the yearbook. Strange that I, Imogen Malley, have a Boy Topic to discuss. It's not exactly peach fuzz and roses, as Mom would say, more like battered knuckles and internal bleeding, but it's mine. When no picture of Ricky pops up in the official class-photo section, we check the index, too. He's not in it.

He must be new this year.

After Mom, Hunter, and Hannah leave, I knock on Dad's office door.

"Come in," he calls.

He's sitting at the computer, files spread out on his desk, a mug of coffee and an empty box of donut holes beside him. My eyes fixate on that empty box.

"Hey."

"Hey there," he says. "How'd you sleep?"

"Okay. Hey, Dad, I was thinking. Since I'm not doing martial arts for a while, do you maybe want to do some weight training with me?"

He barely looks up from the computer. "Sorry, kiddo, I don't have time right now. I'm on deadline."

"Maybe in a few hours? Just, like, a twenty-minute break. I'll do it with you. I'll help you—"

He's shaking his head. "I don't think so. Not today. Too much to do."

It doesn't have to be right now, I repeat to myself. *It doesn't have to be today.* But I can't form the words.

When Dad got home from the hospital last year, we thought we'd have to move, but it was cheaper to cash in his insurance and remodel the house. Besides adding ramps to the front and back doors and a lift onto the minivan so he can still drive, Mom and Dad moved their bedroom into the first-floor den and converted the garage into a gym for Dad's physical therapy.

I'm the only one who uses it.

We have a punching bag, a full-length mirror, a bar along the wall (just like at Tae Kwon Do), and a used elliptical machine. It's like the weaker Dad gets, the stronger I get, but if I could take all of my strength and give it to him, I would.

Today I only pretend to work out in the garage. I blast "Flux" from Bloc Party, my standard workout song, and I give the punching bag a couple kicks out of frustration. But I'm too tired to exercise.

(Maybe that's how Dad feels. Is that how Dad feels?

No.

He doesn't even play his guitar anymore.)

Despite my awkwardness around Dad, the rest of the day passes quickly. We're twin slugs, basically, ordering in heaps of food from the Indian place a few blocks over. I try curry chicken with naan and remember eating something like it at DJ's once.

I put lots of vegetables on Dad's plate, but he only eats half of them.

On Thursday, my first day back at school, I almost expect to be welcomed by a Shitty Committee: all the smokers, druggies, and pseudo-gangbangers who get into fights and terrify the administration. "One of us, one of us," they'll chant.

Hunter offers me a ride in, but I decide to walk. I need the exercise; I haven't worked out in days and my legs feel tight. I make a detour past the train tracks and tilt in close when one whooshes by, even though the sound hurts my ears and the dirt and wind rip up my eyes.

When Hunter and I were kids, we loved playing hobos. We put bandannas on our heads and tied some to sticks and put stuffed animals inside, and we wore our dirtiest ripped jeans and smudged our faces with mud.

Dad thought we were dressing up like cleaning ladies. He told us it wasn't nice to make fun of people.

Mom told us the train tracks were not a good place to play.

After Current Events (which is like a mutant growth sprouting from the forehead of History for Dummies), I have study hall, i.e., counseling with Mrs. Hamilton. I make it all the way to her office before I admit to myself I'm not going in. The crack's still there in the display case in the hall. They've swapped my newspaper photo with a newer headline, probably so they don't accidentally glorify my punch, but they haven't gotten around to fixing the glass.

I picture Mrs. Hamilton at her desk, glancing at her clock on the wall and wondering where I am. I picture me and Ricky sitting there on Monday, laughing together, and I can't go in. I picture Ricky's head hitting the display case and causing that crack. I don't blame him for wanting to get the hell away from me, but if I can't talk about the diner with Ricky, I don't want to talk about it at all.

Mom's all over me when I get home.

"Your counselor called, said you never showed up. She blocked the time off for you, sweetheart."

"It's voluntary, and I don't want to go," I say, opening a bag of chips and shoving a fistful in my mouth. One less thing for Dad to eat. I used to think chips were disgusting, all greasy cholesterol, free radicals, blah blah blah. I used to eat carrots and peanut butter if I needed a snack after school or before TKD, something with protein. I used to think I was better than this, but now I know better. I *am* this. I am exactly this.

"I think you should reconsider," says Mom, staring at my hand as it goes back into the bag of chips for more, crinkling the bag and emerging coated in grease and crumbs. "I think talking to someone, a professional, about what happened is a good idea."

"Talking doesn't change anything." My tongue snakes out and licks my lips.

"It might change the way you feel."

I grab a third fat fistful before she yanks the bag away.

On Friday, I find a piece of notebook paper, folded a zillion times so it's thick and triangular, shoved into the grate of my locker.

The paper is ink stained, the note written in messy, back-slanted cursive, a scribble I will cherish forever.

It says, "I liked the star cookies best. Meet me at Mrs. H's?"

I glance down the hallway, both directions, to see if anyone's watching me. I could pretend I never saw the note. It could have fallen out and been kicked down the hallway until it landed in the janitor's swept-up pile of trash.

But it didn't fall out.

It wasn't kicked down the hallway.

Ricky's giving me a second chance. I take off jogging, backpack slamming against my shoulder blades.

Mrs. Hamilton pretends it's no big deal I've decided to show up. Must be reverse psychology. She doesn't want to scare me away by being overly enthused.

Ricky and I sit across from each other. I'm breathing hard from my sprint. He's still got a black eye, but his nose is back to normal for the most part. I shudder thinking of the damage I could have done. His gorgeous face, shifted and rearranged beneath his skin.

He wears a blue T-shirt that reveals his muscular arms, the word "Marines" stretched tightly across his chest. I can't stop looking at him, just drinking him in, especially his rich, kind eyes. They're brown like maple leaves, with gold filaments inside that make me think of bonfires flickering, warm and inviting. I'm so much less anxious in his presence.

Is it the same for him? Is that why he invited me, why he's been drawing me in his sketchbook?

"I understand you and Ricky had a long talk and that you've cleared the air since Monday," Mrs. Hamilton says.

Um, no. But I'm not about to clarify. I glance over at Ricky and then back at Mrs. Hamilton, trying to sound confident. "Yeah, we talked it out."

She holds my gaze for a moment, then adds, "So you both feel comfortable with a joint counseling session?"

"Yes," I say immediately, then blush.

"Very good. Well, Ricky was just telling me it's hard for him to concentrate in class."

"If someone drops a book or the teacher slams the door shut, it sounds like a gun blast," Ricky says, his voice kind of flat. "But if the teacher *doesn't* close and lock the door, I constantly picture a gunman walking inside, so I'm screwing up in classes where the door is open the whole time."

Mrs. Hamilton makes a note of that; I bet she'll privately ask those teachers to close and lock their doors. I hope they do.

It's my turn, I guess, but I don't know what to add. I'm probably getting F pluses in most of my classes, but not because I think a gunman is going to come through the door. Maybe if Daryl had been a teenager I would feel that way, but twenty-eight is too old for me to associate him with a school shooter.

Mrs. Hamilton says it'll be helpful if we go through the events of the diner in detail, step-by-step, a little more each week until we've covered the whole night, but I don't want to do that. I can't even do it by myself, in my thoughts. I always stop when I get to the point where the cops show up. The wall around that memory is getting higher; I can't see over it.

She wants us to try breathing techniques, but I already *know* breathing techniques. She wants us to try meditating, but I already *know* how to meditate.

"I'll tell you anything about how I feel," I say at last. "But I can't, um, talk about certain details because I don't remember them."

My gaze darts back and forth between Ricky and Mrs. Hamilton. Their faces are open, encouraging.

"So, um . . . I guess I feel . . . like nothing I do matters. If I eat junk food or watch TV all day instead of exercising, it doesn't matter." I trip over the words, trying to get them out quickly while they still make sense inside my head. "All the things I was before and all the things I thought were important didn't stop this from happening. So what does it matter?"

When the bell rings, I get up, but Mrs. Hamilton says, "Imogen, you have lunch now, right? Can you stay a bit longer?"

I was hoping for a moment alone with Ricky, so I could apologize in person, and find out what's going on with him.

"Imogen?" she repeats.

"Yeah, I can stay."

Ricky's already out the door anyway. Opportunity lost.

"Tell me a little about your family."

Why? "Um, my older brother, Hunter, is a senior. My mom is a concierge, and my dad's a writer."

"How'd your parents take your suspension?" Mrs. Hamilton asks.

"Okay, I guess."

"Your dad's disabled, right? That's why he couldn't pick you up on Monday?"

"He has type two diabetes and he's supposed to be on a diet, but—" I clam up. I've already said more than I intended to.

"But what?" she asks.

"Nothing."

Mrs. Hamilton starts over. "What did your parents think about you getting your black belt?"

I shrug.

"I'll bet they were proud," Mrs. H. says.

"My dad didn't come to my black belt test." I look away and tap out a rhythm with my fingers on the edge of her desk.

"Oh? How come?"

"'Cause Glenview Martial Arts doesn't have an elevator."

She nods. "That must have been really disappointing for both of you."

It killed me that he wasn't there. I didn't really stop to consider what it did to him.

"It wasn't his fault," I say quickly. But I guess I *did* sort of blame him, at the time; if he had taken better care of himself, he could've been there. But telling Mrs. H. this would sound monstrous.

One of his toes had to be amputated after a fungal infection turned gangrenous. His foot could be next; both of them are numb and tingling, making it difficult to walk. If you get diabetes after the age of forty, it takes eleven years off your life.

Talking about him feels like a betrayal. I'll talk about the diner; that's fair game, as long as Ricky's here, too. But my family's different. They need to be protected.

At lunch, with only fifteen minutes left in the period, I scan the cafeteria for a place to sit. I look for Ricky until I remember he's a senior and doesn't have the same lunch period.

Hannah and DJ are at band rehearsal. Not like DJ would be sitting with me anyway, apparently.

Shelly's sitting by herself near the window, five steps from the exit, which is a good spot because you can see everyone coming and going and, if necessary, plan an escape route.

My fake heart pulses madly.

Shelly Eppes, in the flesh, wearing her faded gray cashmere ballet wrap—a gift from her grandmother—and holding her lunch bag, which is nylon with *Aqua Teen Hunger Force* characters on it. I used to covet it.

It's been five weeks since I've acknowledged her existence in any way.

"Is it okay if I . . . ," I murmur, hovering at her table.

She kicks the chair opposite her, the least possible effort to invite me to sit. Good enough for me.

"Sucks, doesn't it. Everyone turning on you," she says softly. There are big pauses between everything she says. "You were right, by the way. Hunter never called me."

I swallow.

"What bothered me was that you never did, either," she says.

It's cool outside, and the heating grate is at my feet, so my lower half is too hot and my upper half is too cold. I breathe onto the window and watch it fog up.

I look down at what passes for my lunch today: a brownie, Flamin' Hot Cheetos, and two cans of pop, all stolen from Dad's stash. The old me would have gagged. I'm sure Shelly is grossed out, too. We used to cook together on Sunday nights, great big bowls of pasta primavera, and bring the food to school throughout the week to reheat. For us, school was beside the point—the day job. Our real lives were before and after, with goals and dreams that surpassed anything contained within these walls.

"Hannah and Deej still eat in the band room?" She nods her head in that general direction.

"Yeah. Wind-ensemble practice. And DJ's not allowed to hang out with me anymore," I add, rolling my eyes. "Because I might snap or something. So."

"Well, that makes two of us."

"Wait, what? DJ's not *allowed* to hang out with you? I thought she just, you know, didn't want to," I say.

"She told her parents I had sex, which is of course the ultimate evil no-no. And I'm pretty sure she does the slut cough whenever she sees me."

"You're not a slut," I say, surprised.

"I know that," she snaps.

"I can't believe DJ blabbed to her parents." I didn't even tell *my* parents about the Hunter-Shelly Horror. I just let them think we'd drifted apart. "What's wrong with her?"

If I keep asking questions, maybe I can keep our conversation going a little bit longer.

"Sex and violence," Shelly says, holding up her bottled water for a mock toast. "That's us."

She taps her bottled water to my can of pop, and I feel disgusted about what I'm filling my body with: toxic syrup and empty calories and endless lists of synthetic ingredients. I want to trade with her, take her bottled water and down it in one gulp, cleanse my insides, every vessel and vein. Maybe then I'll get my old heart back.

"I got your text," I say. "Thanks."

"Yeah, I wasn't sure you'd take my calls, but there's something I want to tell you," Shelly adds.

I'm about to respond—I'm dying to hear what she has to say—but before I can, the bell rings and she gets up and walks away, her back straight and graceful as always, gliding along like a slide ruler, perfectly perpendicular to the floor.

Hunter performed the Shelly-ectomy with surgical precision, no anesthesia. Is it possible I could still graft her back on, restore the ampersand between our names like a bridge?

As much as I've missed Shelly, I've missed Shelly&Imogen even more.

After school, I'm determined to find Ricky, but I don't have to look far; he's waiting for me near my locker, one of his legs bent, one old sneaker pressed flat against the wall, the way we're not supposed to stand because it leaves a mark.

"Why'd you cover for me?" I ask. "Why'd you tell Mrs. Hamilton we're friends?"

He launches himself off the wall, and I meet him halfway to my locker. "Listen, the way you punched me—it was crazy," he says.

I look down. "I know. But I didn't—" I break off. "I'm *really* sorry," I concede.

He waves it off. "That's not what I mean. I've never been punched like that. I mean, I've been in fights, I've been hit, but never like that."

I forget guys live in a world where some other guy might actually haul off and hit them at any moment. Girls don't really have to worry about their friends doing that. We have other ways of inflicting pain.

"It was like a brick wall," Ricky continues. "You know how in cartoons they see stars and birds chirping and shit? That was me."

I'm proud, but I don't want to come off that way. It's disrespectful of Grandmaster Huan. Although, in another way, it's the best compliment anyone could give me.

Ricky and I lock eyes, searching for the intensity of what we felt that night in the diner. The rush of not knowing if we'd be alive five minutes from now.

It was a high I never asked for, but now I can't forget it, because it was the last time I felt anything other than numbness. Looking in Ricky's eyes changes that. It pulls a thread inside me that unspools faster and faster until I feel a ball of heat hovering inside my belly.

I watch his lips while he says, "I want you to teach me how to fight."

13

"THE MOST IMPORTANT THING TO REMEMBER IS THAT IT'S not your fist that's punching."

"Are you already Zening out on me?"

We're in the garage gym at my house, both clad in sweatpants and tank tops (me with a sports bra underneath), facing the mirror along the wall.

Ricky can probably fight on the level of an orange or purple belt; he's taken boxing classes and works out once a week. He also plays a lot of basketball with friends from his old school.

I want to peel off his tank top and see what his chest looks like.

Wow, okay, backtrack for a second.

Let's see . . .

During the week that we've been meeting here after school for lessons, I've learned a lot about him. He and his mom moved here from Lake Bluff in May. Mrs. Alvarez is running for Congress next fall, and she thinks she has a better chance of winning in a different (read: poorer) district. That's why they live with his *abuelita*. Funny—and/or disturbingly racist—how I considered Ricky's apartment building to be in a not-okay part of town when really it's not that far from my neighborhood, and they moved there deliberately. God only knows what Ricky thinks of my block.

His dad, the marine, won't be home until Thanksgiving. His *abuelita* could've sold her place a long time ago and lived in style with Ricky's parents in Lake Bluff, but she's stubborn and likes her independence. Ricky wasn't too happy about the move, considering he used to live in one of the nicest suburbs of Chicago.

Some of Mrs. Alvarez's opponents say she's cheating the system by moving her campaign a few miles away and pretending to be someone she's not, but she says, "*familia* is the most important thing to me." She wants to serve the community where she grew up, where her mother lives, blah blah, rah rah, political memoir. But his old school is probably better than Glenview High, so that's not really serving *Ricky*. I don't know. He didn't say all that last stuff, but he didn't have to.

It felt nice learning about him, little details I could fold up and place in my pocket to take out later and examine.

I ask why he was at the diner last month. He says he was filling out an application for a part-time job; his mom thought it'd be good for him. She doesn't believe in free rides. He has to pay his own way for everything.

"But now it's closed and I don't have to work there," he says. "Score!"

I know it's horrible, but we both laugh. Like, hysterically. I never thought I'd get to hear it again, our laughter commingling, twisting together like ribbons and rising.

I usually have crushes on the cute, thin Justin Timberlake / Hayden Christensen types with fair skin and high cheekbones, but after being around Ricky four straight days after school, I'm thinking of converting for him.

Ricky with his warm maple eyes and his cute face that's almost too boyish for his tall body and broad shoulders. Ricky with the contagious laugh who shares my macabre sense of humor.

Ricky, the only one who understands.

And did I mention his muscles? 'Cause *damn*.

So far I've taught him stances and three types of kicks: front-straight rising, front snap, and roundhouse. The sweatpants factor is seriously distracting me—we're just one drawstring pull away from seeing underwear.

Focus, focus!

Apparently Hunter's not the only sex fiend in this family.

The only way I know how to teach anyone anything is by duplicating Grandmaster Huan's class. So we go through all the motions, the routine I could do in my sleep: twenty laps around the edges of the mat, twenty jumping jacks, twenty arm rotations, twenty hip rotations, and twenty seconds of leg stretches, each side. That's the warm-up. Ricky's not even winded, which makes two of us. We're well matched.

I skip the part where you bow to the flags and teachers and all that, and as a result I blank on what to do next. Normally we'd do some light gymnastics and practice how to fall, so you don't break your wrist or your neck if you're shoved or thrown.

But Ricky doesn't want to learn that stuff.

I don't really blame him, so I move into a horse stance in front of the mirror to demonstrate a proper punch, which is when he tells me I'm Zening out on him.

"It's not that," I reply. "I just don't know any other way to explain this. It's not your fist that delivers the punch. It's the fact that you pull your other hand back at the same time. It's the torque, the twist of your body, catapulting through your punching hand, that gives it strength." I grab air in my left fist, yank it back to my side, shift my weight, and throw a punch with my right, all while giving a *kiyap*. Ricky watches me intently in the mirror, like he's committing my words and movements to memory.

"Yelling isn't for show," I add, before he can ask. "It's to force yourself to exhale when you land the punch. It also startles your opponent." I bring both hands back to my sides. "And that's how someone like me can knock out someone like you," I say.

"Wait, who said anything about knocking me out?" He looks annoyed for a second, but then he grins. "Okay, almost. My feet *might* have left the ground."

The truth is, we're not here for the same reason.

He wants a shortcut to black belt territory, which is impossible, and I want to know what it feels like to be in a real fight, the kind I was denied at the diner.

I'm training a worthy opponent. I'm going to teach him all the nasty stuff we never get to do, and then I'm going to unleash him on me.

It's too soon to tell Ricky what I've got planned, though. Today we'll just practice punching in front of the mirror, switching left and right until our arms ache. We do this for half an hour. He never shows signs of boredom.

I correct him a few times, pulling his shoulders back. "Don't let your shoulders follow your arms or turn sideways; keep them level."

"How will I know if I'm doing it right?" he says.

"Well, give it a try," I tell him. "Punch me."

He snorts. "Yeah, right."

"I'm serious. Punch my arm. I'll tell you if it hurts."

He hems and haws. "Nah, I'll just use the punching bag."

"I've been doing martial arts half my life; I can take it. And don't you want revenge?"

"I can't just punch you," he insists.

"Well, I'm not gonna show you anything else if you don't."

He balls his fist and lurches toward me, completely disregarding everything I've just taught him, so we have to start over.

I teach him to twist his fist at the last second, to add extra power, and to square his shoulders so the center of his body is an immovable block at all times, no matter what his arms are up to.

"Try again," I say.

"Are you sure?"

"Just do it!"

Still he hesitates!

I roll my eyes. "Here." I punch him in the ribs.

He coughs and staggers—"Oof"—and when he straightens up again, his eyes have clouded over with rage. Before I can express any glee at his transformation, he twists at the waist and pops me in the upper arm.

Freaking ow!!

"Yes." I choke out my words. "That was good. You got it." My arm throbs like hell, the muscle exploding beneath my skin. While Ricky's trying to decide if he should be proud or horrified, I drop in a spin and sweep his legs out, cracking his shins like dominos and knocking him to the floor.

He grunts when his back hits the mat. I crawl over him to gloat, and he reaches up to grab my wrists and pull me down.

We look at each other and my gaze drops to his lips. I'm hovering above his body, my arms propping me up, shaking with the effort of not collapsing on top of him. I wonder what it would be like to let my arms drop, to place my head on his chest or slide my legs through his. But he's not here for that. He's here because he wants to learn what I *know*, not what I don't know; and what I don't know about kissing could fill a book.

Besides, what if we kissed, and then he didn't come back? Hanging out with him in the garage is the only thing I look forward to. I can't risk it just because I'm curious, or horny, or whatever. That's the kind of boner-headed thing Hunter would do, and if there's one person I refuse to emulate, it's Hunter.

I know I'm not imagining the heat between us, though. Ricky feels it, too, and he laughs. It's a nervous habit of his, he explained to me earlier. He didn't mean to laugh about my black belt that day. It's kind of annoying, but it's flattering, too: I make him nervous.

I roll over on my back so we're side by side, staring at the ceiling. Not touching.

"Do you have a boyfriend?" he says.

Ha, please. But I guess it's a good sign that he can't tell. We don't look at each other; we both keep looking at the ceiling.

"No," I manage to get out with a straight face. "You?"

"No boyfriend," he teases.

I roll my eyes. "Girlfriend?"

"There was someone at my old school, but we didn't want to do long distance."

A few miles equals long distance? But this is good news. It's great news.

"Cool," I say, but we still don't look at each other.

"Nice weights," Ricky says, pointing to the corner. "Brand-new?"

"They're my Dad's." Six months old. Never used.

"Oh, okay. I won't touch them."

"I could ask him."

"No worries. Can you do this again tomorrow?" he says.

I look over and see him watching me. His eyes are warm copper medallions.

I smile and he smiles back.

14

OKAY, SO WE DIDN'T KISS, BUT BY THE TIME WE SAY GOOD night, there's an aching, split-orange lump on my arm I enjoy even more. And we have plans for tomorrow, which means there's no one he'd rather spend his Friday evening with. Date night.

I'm feeling so good after dinner that I ask if I can go over to Shelly's.

"Is her banishment lifted?" says Hunter dryly.

"What do you care?"

"Tell her congratulations from me."

"I'll be sure not to do that," I snap.

"Tone it down," Dad says.

"I think it's nice you're seeing her. Say hi for us," Mom says.

I call first, like I'm making an appointment. I never used to do that—I'd just walk or bike over—but after not speaking for over a month, the least I can do is make sure she's okay with me being there. When I dial her phone, I feel like I'm tapping in the numbers to a code that will open a door to my old life.

Shelly says to come over in ten minutes because she and her mom are still eating.

When I ring the doorbell, Mrs. Eppes answers, and the first thing she does is wrap me in a warm quilt of a hug. It reminds me of the nights I spent living here the week Dad was in the hospital. I stayed in the guest room (although as soon as Mrs. Eppes went to sleep, Shelly waved me into her room and we sat up all night and talked). We were sort of mean to her mom, in retrospect. Like, when we made tacos for lunch, we served Mrs. Eppes one with tons of hot sauce without warning her. We also rigged the top of her bedroom door with a crapload of stuffed animals so every time she walked in they'd fall on her in clumps. I don't know why. It seemed hilarious at the time.

The weird thing is, I rarely hug my own mom, but with Shelly's mom it's normal and comforting. I'm glad she's there to play third-party moderator during my transition back into Shelly's life, if indeed that's what tonight is going to be. With her there, Shelly and I are not likely to start yelling at each other.

Mrs. Eppes asks if I want some tea, which I do, and after giving her an update on my family, I rinse out my mug and follow Shelly up to her room, where I take my usual beanbag seat on the floor. Her room seems different. The Green Day posters are gone and I'm pretty sure the walls have been painted. The collage of photos of her, me, Hannah, and DJ is also gone. Hanging above her bed, with ribbons falling down, is a pair of silky-looking ballet shoes. There's a beautiful, intricate card standing on the bedside table, one of those expensive cards from Papyrus. The décor seems grown-up somehow.

"So how are you *really* doing?" she asks. She knows I've fed her mom a platter of BS, so now she wants the gritty director's cut of the diner scene or the suspension subplot. But instead I tell her I almost kissed Ricky.

I realize as soon as it's out of my mouth what a pathetic non-event it is. All my good feelings from before seem stupid and childish.

"But I guess once you've slept with someone, kissing's not a big deal anyway," I add. I can't push aside her betrayal just because some time has passed or because way worse things have happened to me since then. I can't pretend she didn't ruin our friendship.

"That's not what I'm thinking!" she says.

"Congratulations on achieving your goal, I guess. Third on the list, was it?" My face burns and my sore arm vibrates and my fingers itch. The feeling spreads to my throat and makes it difficult to speak. I have the urge to tear open her beanbag chair with my teeth and watch all the beads pour out.

She doesn't respond.

"Will you just tell me one thing?" I ask.

She nods.

"Was it always going to be Hunter?" I whisper. "Was he the goal all along?"

"No," she says emphatically. "I swear. You *know* he wasn't. It just happened. I didn't plan it—where are you going?" Shelly moves to block the door. As if I couldn't steamroll over her. "Are you leaving already?"

"You knew it would wreck everything between us."

"You probably won't believe me, but I didn't. I really didn't. It wasn't about you."

"But you chose him over me."

"I didn't think it was a choice. I didn't think it was either/or. Look, it was selfish of me, and I'm sorry. But what you did was worse."

"Me?!"

"A couple days, I get. A week, I get. You had every right to be pissed. But you guys ignored me for *over a month.* I spent every single lunch in my car—"

Crying. DJ saw her once. *Good,* I thought at the time. Now I feel ashamed.

"Five weeks, five days a week, a ghost in the hall, invisible," she whispers. "You'd look right through me, like I wasn't there, like I'd *never* been there, like we'd *never been friends*. It was so cold."

She sighs and sits down on her bed. Most of us would slump in this situation, but she maintains excellent posture. She's a dancer every second of every day.

"You said there was something you wanted to tell me," I remind her. "In the cafeteria."

"I only auditioned because my aunt in New York said I could live with her. I didn't think I would get in," she says wildly. "But then I did!"

Her sudden excitement makes me nervous. I need to slow this down. "What audition?"

"Manhattan Dance Company, Juniors Program."

I remember us driving to Indiana in August, the last day of Grandmaster Huan's camp, the night we looked at the stars and talked about all the things we were going to do.

"I found out the morning of your birthday," Shelly says, "but I didn't want to steal your thunder. I was going to tell you the next day. But when I went upstairs—I don't even remember why—"

"To get my camera," I grumble.

"—Hunter was there and I just had to tell someone. He was so happy for me. It was just a kiss." Pause. "It was just *supposed* to be a kiss." Another pause. "I know you don't think he's nice, but he's always been nice to me."

"Yeah, he's extra-special nice to all of my friends," I say. "Because he wants to rob the cradle."

"But Imogen, he and I are the same age."

I always forget I'm the youngest person in our grade; my birthday's in August, but my parents got me into first grade a year early. Shelly's birthday is in October; she's turning seventeen, same as Hunter is now. I should probably be a sophomore instead of a junior. Sometimes I wonder if that's why school is so difficult for me—but it probably shouldn't matter.

"So you and Hunter celebrated?" I mutter sarcastically. Shelly stares at me, and I can't keep her gaze for long. "He used you."

"*I* used *him*!" she says, slapping her hand against her bed. "I wanted to have sex before I left. So I wouldn't feel pressure to have it in New York. So when people talked about boyfriends and stuff, I'd have something to say that wouldn't be pretend, that wouldn't be a lie."

"It's not like *Gossip Girl*. Just 'cause they live in New York City doesn't mean they're all sex fiends."

"Having sex doesn't make you a sex fiend," she says.

"I never said it did."

"You act like it."

"What are you talking about?" I'm seriously at a loss.

"When I told you it was my goal, you made me feel like I was a freak for even thinking about it. It was mostly a joke; I was just throwing it out there, but you shut down so fast I couldn't even explain how I felt: like the whole world was passing me by while all I did was go to dance practice, do my homework, study for tests, write for the *Spectator*. No dates, no boyfriends—I've never had that."

"Neither have I—"

"You went on that group date with Hannah and DJ."

"That was nothing—"

"I knew Hunter wouldn't brag to his friends afterward and that he'd still be nice to me. Which he has been. He always says hi to me in the hallway, and he gave me a card on my birthday."

I'm about to say something like, "He gives cards to *all* his fuh-buddies on their birthdays," but then I think, crap. October birthday. What's today's date? The seventh? Her birthday's the fifth.

I missed it.

I get up for a closer look at the card on her bedside table (Was it the only one she got? Oh God.), and I open it. Hunter signed my name as well, pretending it was from both of us. I don't know whether to laugh or cry. It's more than I deserve. Obviously.

I sit next to Shelly on her bed. We're silent for a long time, because what do you say after that?

"So are you gonna go?" My voice trembles. "To New York?"

"I wasn't sure at first if I should accept. I had to get a few more credits completed before I could enroll, and I didn't want to leave my mom by herself or leave you guys, but then you started ignoring me, and so did Hannah and DJ—"

"It's not like I told them to stop calling you," I say. "I don't control them. We were all just pissed."

She doesn't argue. "I leave November first, so . . ."

"Aw, jeez," I say, my eyes filling with tears. I wipe frantically at my face, because it feels manipulative, like I'm crying in front of her to make her feel sorry for me. I swear I'm not.

"In a way I should be thanking you," Shelly says with a shrug. "If we hadn't had our fight, I might have stayed here, which probably would've been the wrong decision."

She shrugs again, but her face looks pinched and small, like maybe she's holding back tears as well. She has a point, though. This is an amazing opportunity for her, and she should take it. She should get to pursue her dream.

And if I'm jealous at all, it's only because she still has a dream.

15

I CANCEL MY "DATE" WITH RICKY THE NEXT DAY BECAUSE who am I fooling? We're not dating. I'm just teaching him martial arts. I'm sure he has better things to do on a Friday night, like hook up with his old girlfriend.

He sounds disappointed, so I quickly mention I'm free Monday.

We resume our lessons all week but keep things strictly professional.

Every night when he leaves, I replay our time together in my head. I can't help it. I like how we are with each other, how quick and funny he makes me feel. I wish we could record our conversations so I could prove it to the rest of the world, show them a side of me that's always been there but had no reason to reveal itself until I met Ricky.

I convince myself that kissing him would've destroyed everything.

When I got my first period a few years ago, Mom made us go out to Fuddruckers to celebrate. It was absolutely horrifying. Hunter took me aside later and told me girls are so brave; he couldn't handle bleeding and not being able to stop it.

Saturday night, one month since the diner, I dream I'm in a bathtub full of blood. The mixture is a foul, pungent, coppery stew. Bits of skin and teeth and brain matter float to the top, rising toward my mouth to gag me. Black fluff from the gunman's ski mask drifts onto my tongue, and for some reason that disturbs me most of all.

"What the hell are you doing, Daryl?"

"Just empty the register! Shut up."

The problem with sleeping on the second floor when your parents are on the first floor is that if you wake up screaming, no one will help you.

Hunter's there in a flash, though, kneeling by my bed.

"You okay?" he whispers, squeezing my hand once, a pacemaker delivering a volt to my imposter heart. "I'm right here."

I can feel matted hair and teeth and chunks of skin in my

mouth, as though they've crossed into our world from the other realm, the place where dreams are, and I grab the plastic wastebasket next to my bed and hurl.

To his credit, Hunter doesn't jump back or run out of the room. He'll make a good dad someday, I guess, since babies are so gross and everything. When I'm finished, he gets a box of tissues and a glass of water from the bathroom and brings them to me.

I'm sweating like a beast.

He perches carefully on the edge of my bed and pats my hair back down. It makes me think of Dad getting the tangles out when I was a kid.

"Thanks. Remember when Dad used to sing us to sleep with his guitar?" I ask.

"Yeah. He was really good," Hunter says, sounding wistful. Or maybe he just sounds that way because I want him to feel the same way I do.

The minute I jolt awake from a nightmare the next night, I ditch my pajamas; pull on a hoodie, sneakers, and jeans; and sneak out of the house.

Our neighborhood's silent and dark, the occasional car with a broken headlight floating by like a shark, slowing down to take a look at me. I've never been out so late by myself, just walking around, past the graffiti-coated bus stops and all-night liquor stores and construction sites—giant pits in the ground where grocery stores used to be.

Someone could attack me.

I have no fear, because I don't care what happens. There's something incredibly freeing in this realization. I *want* someone to attack.

My absence doesn't go unnoticed, however.

"I go out walking after midnight," Hunter sings at breakfast the next morning, tapping his hands against the kitchen table.

I slam my fork down and say with clenched teeth, "You better not tell them."

"Where'd you go?"

"Nowhere."

"I followed you in the car," he crows. "You went to the diner."

"Then why'd you ask, dumbass?" It pisses me off that I had backup. Last night's trek was supposed to be about me doing something potentially dangerous, on my own, and dealing with the consequences, preferably by kicking someone's ass if they jumped me.

Hunter staked out in Mom's freakin' grocery getter, watching me from afar, was not part of that plan.

The diner was a letdown, anyway. Rain pelted the dark windows, and a single streetlamp illuminated the fact that one of the windows was broken. Damp, crumpled leaves had blown inside and scattered along the floor, covering what were probably chalk outlines and bloodstains.

Mostly, though, it was a shuttered building in a quiet, empty lot.

"If you tell them, I'll tell Mom and Dad about you and Shelly Eppes on my birthday," I say, and he looks upset for a second.

"Go ahead," he says with a shrug.

"If you tell them," I say, "I will *never* forgive you."

That shuts him up.

Momentarily.

"What's up with you and Ricky?" he asks.

"None of your business."

"He's been here every day after school for two weeks."

"I'm teaching him martial arts."

"Grappling, on the floor?" Hunter waggles his eyebrows.

"*No.*"

"Do you like him?"

"Not the way *you* like people. We're deeper than that," I insist. "We actually talk to each other, when we're not practicing forms."

He looks at me, scanning my face for hints and clues. "Try the shallow end sometime. You might like it."

On Wednesday, Mrs. Richardson asks me to stay late after Current Events because she's noticed I never participate in class anymore. I want to tell her I barely participate in *life* so it's nothing personal, but then she takes out my homework assignment like it's exhibit A and she's a judge on *Law & Order: Little Shits Unit.*

We have this term-length project (Don't the teachers ever freaking speak to each other? Don't they know we're all reading *Bleak House*?) that requires us to subscribe to the *International Herald Tribune*, in print or online, and select one article per day to paste in a notebook. One per day! Underneath the article, we have to write a summarizing paragraph, a sentence conveying how this international event affects the United States, and a sentence of our own personal response.

My notebook's filled with international disasters. Summary: "Shit happened." How it affects the United States: "Not much." Personal response: "Remind self never to leave the United States."

Apparently this doesn't amuse Mrs. Richardson.

"Besides the off-color language, which the girl I remember from ninth-grade History would never use, your responses are identical for each news story," she points out.

I cross my arms. "Well, that's how I feel."

"You can't just write, 'Japanese people are messed up.' Or 'Italian people are messed up.'"

"But that's how I feel. I mean, look at this article. It says Japanese salarymen get so drunk every night after work there are people whose sole job it is to clean up their puke on the subway trains. That's messed up," I say.

"Your personal responses are fueled by xenophobia."

"No, they're not. I'd say, 'Americans are messed up' if we had to read articles about the U.S. Look, you can't tell me my personal response is *wrong*. It's a personal response. It can't be right or wrong; it's just my response. I can't help how I feel; it's how I *feel*—"

I haven't cried about the diner I have no feelings I'm not human Mom keeps telling me to have a good cry but something in me got turned off like a switch and now other people can tell I'm not normal, I'm heartless.

I confess my fears to Mrs. Hamilton. Not because I want to— Mrs. Richardson blabbed about my psycho reaction to her assignment (so teachers *do* talk to each other when it's juicy gossip).

The weird thing is, when I show up for counseling, Ricky's just leaving. He gives me a tight smile as he walks by.

Why is he seeing Mrs. Hamilton without me?

I tell her about riding to the station; the inside of the squad car covered in plastic wrap; me and my thick, slimy, wet second skin; and the female cop cutting me out of my clothes.

"She sliced through them with scissors, and I kept thinking, 'Who's gonna pay for this shirt?' I wanted to know if I could get a refund for it." My good-enough-for-the-popular-kids shirt. "Who thinks about that stuff when someone has died?"

"You were in shock," Mrs. Hamilton says. "You still are. It's your brain's way of dealing, to focus on smaller things. You can't help what you were thinking, and it doesn't make you a bad person."

Easy for her to say.

"But now I'm confused," she admits, leaning toward me and tapping her chin with her fingertip. "Whenever you've talked about the diner with me, you say you were under the table the whole time."

I nod. "Right."

Low to the ground is comforting; standing up is bad.

"But the cash register was several feet away. If you were under the table the whole time, then why were you covered in blood?"

I pinch my eyes shut, but nothing comes in; no images form a bridge between *under the table* and *not under the table*. There's just shouting, and gunshots, and me in the police car, covered in blood.

"I guess I *wasn't* under the table the whole time. I guess it just felt that way." I look at her. "I mean, I *know* I wasn't, but—" I rub at my arms, moving the skin back and forth, trying to push away my blood-soaked T-shirt, the red tarp of cotton sticking to me. "The blood was real. The blood was real . . ."

She places a hand on my wrist before I can do any damage to my arms.

"It's okay. I know it was real. You don't have to try to remember right now. But I think in the future, remembering will help you recover."

For the rest of October, Ricky and I practice three times a week in the garage, sort of like my old Tae Kwon Do schedule. I don't know what he sees when he looks at me. Our only rule is no marks above the neck or any place a sleeve doesn't cover. When we spar, we don't wear any padding; it's bone against bone. My shins and arms are the color of plums at first, and then rotten mangos. All the bruises of the rainbow.

The "no face" rule isn't much better than the rules of Tae Kwon Do, but I have to live with it if I want Ricky to continue. Sometimes I wonder what the point is, though, if we're not fighting for real. If we're still holding back.

He told me he feels nervous unless he sees me at least once a day, because if he doesn't know firsthand I'm okay, he'll spend his classes wondering if something's happened to me. He's a senior, so we don't even get lunch together. But we pass in the hall at the halfway mark, by my locker, and we look each other in the eyes, just a quick moment that says, "I'm here. You're not alone."

"Mrs. H. asked me something weird," I tell him when we

take a break from practicing in the garage. I'm still confused about seeing him in her office without me, and maybe he wonders the same thing about me. I quickly explain. "I had to see her on my own because I'm failing Current Events."

I pause, giving him the chance to reciprocate and tell me why he was leaving her office when I showed up. But he doesn't take me up on the offer.

"She said, 'If you were under the table the whole time, why were you covered in blood?'"

Ricky doesn't answer right away. "You don't remember?" he says at last.

"It's like I do, but I don't. There's a gap. I was under the table, and then I was in the police car. I know it was bad. I know it all went wrong. I just can't picture it."

I'm standing at the mirror, which faces another mirror on the opposite wall. Ricky stands behind me and murmurs in my ear, "Maybe you shouldn't try. Maybe it's your brain's way of protecting you."

We stare at each other in the wall mirrors, and all our images on down to infinity stare at each other, too. I keep thinking one pair of them might be brave and break away from the rest; maybe one of the Imogens, just one of the hundreds, will turn around and kiss one of the Rickys. I picture the rest of us looking on jealously. If only one pair of us does it, it won't count, it won't have to change anything, it won't risk what we have—our closeness. One version of us could kiss, and the rest of us could still be safe.

I'm wondering if the person to break free of the mirror images will be me or a different Imogen, when—supreme mortification!—Dad interrupts us. At least we have fair warning and can back away from each other as he wheels in.

Dad's wheelchair isn't a sleek, high-tech motorized one. It's all metal footrests and squeaking rubber, because it was supposed to be temporary.

"Nice to meet you, sir," Ricky says, hand outstretched.

Most people become paralyzed around the wheelchair-bound; I've seen adults in the mall overcompensate by pretending they don't see Dad. They're terrified that if they glance over and their gaze lingers for a fraction of a second, it'll be rude. So instead they ignore him, because *that's* realistic. *Even though you're half our height, twice as wide, and blocking the aisle, we don't notice you there. Why would we?*

But Ricky looks right at Dad, the way I wish I could.

Dad shakes his hand and says, "Nice to meet you, too."

"The gym is really well equipped. Thanks for letting me use it," Ricky says.

"Well, that's entirely Imogen's doing. She picked everything out."

"Dad, can we chat later?" I ask, giving Ricky a "Don't contradict me" look. "We're in the middle of something."

Ricky ignores me. "Mr. Malley, I was wondering if I might have your permission to take Imogen out to dinner on Saturday."

Is this actually happening? What are we, an 1800s family?

Dad cracks a smile, removes his glasses, cleans them, and places them back on. His eyes are tiny and then huge again. "Sure. Assuming that's okay with you, honey?" he says to me.

"Uh. Yeah. Sounds good."

And that's how Ricky Alvarez asks me out.

16

ON SATURDAY AFTERNOON, HUNTER INVITES GRETCHEN over to dip me in the beauty vat before Ricky picks me up. Her zillion younger sisters are apparently always begging her for makeovers. Hunter probably thought he was being helpful, but I want Ricky to like me as I am, not as some Franken-girl sewn together by one of Hunter's exes.

"How are you doing these days?" Gretchen asks, flicking through her makeup bag and selecting an eye-shadow brush.

I shrug. Maybe it's too much to hope for, but I want to spend one evening without images from the diner infringing. They're always on the edge of my consciousness, fighting to tear through. If my brain's the arena, my thoughts are the rabid caged dogs in the wings, whipped into a fury. As long as I don't acknowledge them, I can keep them at bay until I go to bed, at which point they show up as nightmares and tear themselves apart.

But while I'm awake, I can drug their food.

Gretchen offers me a couple of outfits to borrow, an *InStyle* magazine, and some perfume samples. My own mascara and blush are good, but I end up borrowing a lipstick and some earrings from her—small enough items so I don't feel fake, but also so I don't make Gretchen feel like her visit was a waste of time.

"Congrats on winning class president," I say as she gathers her items and heads for the door. "I think Hunter voted for you twice. I definitely would've voted for you if I was a senior."

"Thanks," Gretchen says. "It's been good for me, staying so busy. Have fun on your date and don't be a stranger, okay?"

"Okay."

"I'm serious. We should hang out, meet up at Dairy Delight again some night Hunter's working."

Aha. She's still hung up on Hunter. Can't say I'm surprised, but I am a little sad. For a second there, it felt like we might become friends on our own terms.

I shake off the familiar disappointment and try to focus on my date.

By eight o'clock, Ricky and I are seated in a booth at the back of Mr. Yang's Chinese Bistro, inhaling the scent of orange chicken and kung pao peppers as they float by.

Ricky's kind of rocking back and forth in his seat; I don't think he realizes he's doing it.

I immediately flag down the hostess. "Can we get a different table?" I ask.

"Where would you like?"

"Over there," I say, pointing to a spot by a window.

The awkwardness started when Ricky picked me up tonight, because he's never formally rung the doorbell or even come inside the house except to grab water after our garage workouts. I wasn't sure how to act, or why anything should feel like an act to begin with, and I also wasn't sure how dressed up he was going to be. I didn't want to look (a) too casual or (b) not casual enough. I wanted us to match.

He's in jeans and a blazer and a skinny tie, and I'm in a dark-wash jean skirt, tights, and a sweater. I think we look pretty spiff together, but so far the awkwardness hasn't abated.

We sit down at our new table and get our menus. The silence between us is unbearable.

"So! What are you going to order?" I ask, after a prolonged moment spent looking at, but not really seeing, the specials and appetizers. I hate this conversation; it's not even a conversation. It's what people say when they don't know what else to say.

"Not sure yet," he mumbles back.

We should've stayed home. We should've stuck to the pattern. We should be working on sidekicks and palm-heel strikes in our sweatpants and tank tops, not playing dress up and pretend. We're no good at this.

What scares me is how upset the thought makes me. I wanted us to be good at this.

I bet there are no lulls when Hunter goes on a date, maybe because their tongues are busy in other ways. But who wants to kiss if the rest of it's missing? With Ricky, we had "the rest of it" down pat. Or, at least, we did before.

His eyes flit around the room, darting this way and that—and any time the door opens and another customer walks in, he watches them for a while, his leg bouncing.

At this point in the evening, the female dater supposedly sets the tone for the night, based solely on what she orders. Salad? Lame; possible eating disorder. Lobster? Expensive, which means either bitchy or slutty. It's so unfair and ridiculous.

I tell this to Ricky, and he squints his eyes. "You better choose the right thing," he says fake menacingly, snapping his menu shut. "Or this night is over."

I suck some water into my straw and pretend I'm going to squirt it at him. He barely reacts. What's happening to us?

Right after we order, there's a crash in the kitchen; someone's dropped a bunch of plates. Ricky jumps, knocking over his water.

"Are you okay?" I ask.

A waiter comes by to mop up the spill, and Ricky bolts out of his chair.

"I can't—I can't sit here anymore," he says.

I stand, too, tossing my napkin to the table. "It's all right, it's—"

"I can't *be* here anymore."

"Let's go outside for a second." I turn to the waiter. "We'll be right back."

I take Ricky's hand in mine, and we move outside. That's how easy it turned out to be: grabbing onto his hand as an impulse, without thinking. In fact, I don't even realize what I've done until he lets my hand go so he can drag his fingers through his hair.

"Sorry," he says, the word a puff of white in the cold night air. "Fuck! This isn't how I wanted this night to go. This was supposed to be normal. I wanted to give you a normal night."

"Hey," I say gently, looking at him until he looks back. Strange how we spent minutes (hours, years) looking at each other at the diner, giving strength to each other, but now he has trouble and I have to coax his trust out of him. It's my job to coax it out of him.

Our eyes meet at last, and a jolt of longing—to see him better, to see him okay—gives me confidence to speak. I can do this for him. Maybe I've been waiting to do this the whole evening. "It's us. It's you and me. I don't care about any of this stuff. We can go home; we can go back to my gym and just work out if you want. I don't care. We don't have to do 'normal things.' We can just be us. What we have isn't normal, and I don't see why it should be."

It's better than normal, I think.

He sits down at the curb and I join him. He reaches for my hand, and I stroke his knuckles with my thumb until he relaxes. His hand is warm, a comfort against the chilly air.

I guess once you hold hands that first time, it's never strange to keep doing it. (Would kissing be the same?)

"I haven't eaten in a restaurant since that night," Ricky says. "Have you?"

"Not really," I tell him. "Just Dairy Delight, where my brother works. But I freaked out at the movies."

"Well, that's better than me. I don't go anywhere anymore. Just school, home, and your place. I even stopped playing basketball with my friends. I don't go anywhere, and I don't do anything, and just making myself walk in there was like . . . I don't know. Like tempting fate, like saying, 'Come and get me. I'm a sitting duck again.' Every time the door opened, every time I saw a guy come in, didn't matter who it was, I thought,

He's packing and he's going to open fire, and we're all just *sitting here*."

"Ricky . . ."

"I know," he sighs. "It's stupid."

"No, it's not."

"Mrs. Hamilton told me teenagers are resilient, that we'll bounce back," he scoffs. "And I'm thinking, Okay. *When?*"

I don't remember Mrs. Hamilton saying that, but I've heard the theory before. That the younger you are, the quicker you can normalize an event and move on, because you don't know any other way of life. It just becomes a small part of your narrative as the years go by. But it seems to me the younger you are when something bad happens to you, the longer you have to carry it with you.

Why couldn't we have witnessed a shooting when we were, like, seventy-seven?

"She also said it could get worse before it gets better," Ricky mutters. "But how could it get worse? Like, what, I won't be able to leave the house at all?"

I have no answer for him.

"Are you hungry, or should we ditch this place?" I ask.

"Do you mind if we take the food back to my *abuelita*'s?"

"Are you kidding? I love her."

After we grab our coats from the hooks at the front of the restaurant, Ricky holds the door open, and DJ, Philip, and DJ's parents come in as we're going out. DJ stares right at me, and her eyes widen. She looks like she's about to say something, but then she glances at her parents, who are staring straight ahead, and doesn't say a word.

"Hi, Imogen," says Philip, nodding to me, and DJ elbows him. "What? Oh, sorry."

"You were really nice to my dad," I tell Ricky once we're settled in at his place, unpacking our takeout bags at the kitchen table. Cashew chicken for me, crab Rangoon and noodles for him.

Halloween decorations dot the fridge, small things like black cats and pumpkin magnets. Ricky looks much better now that we're back in familiar surroundings.

"Are most people mean to him?" Nervous laughter.

"No, not exactly mean, but . . . a lot of people look past him or try to get out of the conversation as soon as possible."

He shrugs. "I'm kind of used to seeing guys in wheelchairs. Some of my dad's friends are war vets who've lost limbs and things like that. What happened with him?" Ricky's voice is kind, more curious than anything else, but then his mother walks in, so I'm saved from answering.

Mrs. Alvarez is shorter in person, but otherwise her campaign photos are accurate: she's this well-lit poster come to life, all cascading, curly dark hair, with Ricky's same brown-and-gold-flecked eyes, and she has the biggest, friendliest smile I've ever seen.

"You are Ricky's *novia*, yes?" she says, leaning down to kiss my cheek and give my shoulder a squeeze. "So nice to meet you."

Am I his *novia*? Ricky's girlfriend? The thought makes me giddy for a second. The nicest part is that Ricky's apparently felt that way for a while, long enough to tell his mother so, even though this is our first date and we've only held hands.

"Hi, Mrs. Alvarez. Nice to meet you, too."

"My mother says hello, by the way. She's at her book club."

"Sorry we missed her."

"I'm curious, how are you guys eating that, exactly?" she says.

Ricky and I are sitting at the same side of the table, our plates and chairs smushed together, holding hands beneath the table. In our free hands we've got one half of a pair of chopsticks each, and we're working together to scoop the food up and into our mouths, one piece at time. It's taking forever, but we refuse to stop holding hands. We're like those paper dolls joined at the hand, and to separate us would require a severing of limbs, and you couldn't even say whose because they've merged.

"It's a synchronized, coordinated effort," I say. "Want some?"

She looks down at our plates, all the food mixed together in a messy pile, and demurs. "I was going to make hot chocolate, so I think I'll pass."

I worry she's going to ask about my suspension, but either Ricky and his *abuelita* have kept that fact from her, or she considers it old news.

After we clear our plates, Mrs. Alvarez pours hot chocolate into a mug for me straight from a saucepan. I learn hot chocolate doesn't mean warm chocolate; it means hot peppers, like eye-popping *caliente*-hot. It's rich and delicious and makes my tongue throb and my pores sweat. I feel like running out into the cold air and spinning around with my mouth open.

"What are you working on tonight, Mom?" says Ricky.

She chuckles. "Translation: 'Go back to what you're working on, Mom.'"

"I didn't say that," Ricky protests.

"It's okay. I'll leave you be. I'm putting together an outreach program for the women's center on Halstead." She turns to me. "You have any older siblings?"

I nod.

"Are they eighteen years old?" she asks.

"Mama," Ricky groans.

"He'll be eighteen next year."

"Tell him to vote," she says with a grin.

"All right, you're done here," Ricky teases.

"Hunter voted twice in our school election," I offer.

"Tell him *not* to vote twice." She flashes her megawatt Anne Hathaway smile again. "Enjoy your night. I'll be in the den."

After Mrs. Alvarez leaves, Ricky cracks open his fortune cookie. I miss the feel of his hand in mine.

"What's it say?" I lean in and bat my eyelashes.

"'You'll be sucker punched in the face by a really cute girl.' Huh. Sometimes they predict the past."

I blush. No one's ever called me cute before.

We don't say much on the drive home. When Ricky parks his car in my parents' driveway, I'm afraid our earlier awkwardness from the start of the evening has returned. He turns off the car, and we move toward each other. Part of me thinks, "I'm not ready!" and maybe I'm transparent or maybe he's not ready either because instead of kissing me, he pulls me into a tight hug.

Our hearts punch toward each other in opposite syncopation, trading beats, sharing the burden. Where one pushes, the other pulls—back and forth like saws.

I lay my head against his chest and listen to his heartbeat. I recognize the rhythm, steady and strong. It's my heart, inside his chest. My heart, my heart! It's been with him the whole time. I think they got swapped at the diner, and now he's keeping it safe for me. The closer I stay to him, the closer I am to my true heart. I don't expect to trade back. I just want visitation rights. His arms feel firm around me.

For the first time since the diner, I am completely calm, like I might be okay someday. Not yet, but someday. Like by being together, we've not only survived, we've won, and if one of us lets go, the other will drop.

The next day, Sunday, is Halloween. *Cosmo* would disapprove, since it's way too soon after our first date, but I text Ricky in the morning and ask if he wants to watch DVDs with me and Hannah. I'm thinking *It's the Great Pumpkin, Charlie Brown*; *Paranormal Activity*; and a third to be named later. That way it seems casual, like an afterthought; "I already have these plans, care to join?"

He responds right away with a smiley emoticon.

The weird part is that Hunter insists on staying in, too.

"Hi, Hannah, what's up?" he says, all loud and friendly, bounding down the stairs like a Labrador puppy when she arrives. Ricky's already in the living room.

"I'm surprised you're not out bobbing for boobs at some Halloween party," she says.

Holy fuh! I had no idea Hannah could be so funny. Maybe DJ censors her.

Hunter looks between us for a moment before heaving this put-upon sigh. "You're still giving me a hard time about Imogen's birthday? You're as bad as my sister."

"I'm worse. I'm your worst nightmare," she says, making her eyes go wide and crazy looking. I sputter with laughter.

Undeterred, Hunter follows us to the other room and lies down, propped up by his elbows, next to Hannah on the floor (Ricky and I called the couch). Hannah snickers at him and tells him to sit on his hands.

On the couch, Ricky and I sit on separate cushions but close enough that our knees and the sides of our fingers occasionally brush against each other's. The places we touch are the only parts of me that are warm, but it's enough. Somehow I can feel it everywhere.

Our movies are interrupted every couple of minutes by trick-or-treaters. We alternate who gets up and deals with them, and when Ricky returns from his round, he tells me there's a girl outside who wants to say hi to me.

I open the front door and almost don't recognize Taylor, my favorite student from summer camp, even when she takes off her Lisa Simpson mask; she looks taller and doesn't duck her face or mumble when she talks. Her posture's improved, and there's a core of confidence fused to her spine.

She knows this is my house because I had her over one time after class when her mom was late to pick her up.

I smile and invite her in.

"Is he your boyfriend?" she stage-whispers, nodding her head wildly in the direction of the living room.

"He's hot, right?" I stage-whisper back.

She nods, then speaks in a normal voice. "I'm testing for my yellow belt this weekend," she says proudly. "Do you want to come?"

My smile falters. "Oh, uh, I'm not allowed."

"I talked to Grandmaster Huan. He said it's okay for you to be there just to watch. So do you want to come? Maybe we could go over the *poomse* beforehand. There's this one part I need your help with: when you do the lower block, I always forget which way I'm supposed to turn."

My shy little Taylor's become a chatterbox. She demonstrates the problem move, and I gently correct her. "Think of it like the symbols on the Korean flag. You know, the black bars on the lower left? They correspond to the direction you turn. If you've already done the first rung, you know it's time to turn this way."

"Cool, thanks."

We look at each other for a second. I fight the urge to ask who else from camp signed up for the fall session. It's none of my business, not anymore.

"Well, I should probably go," Taylor says, glancing outside. "My friends are at the next house and they're gonna wonder where I am."

"Hey, does Grandmaster Huan still say, 'Be. More. Natural' whenever you're doing the most unnatural move ever?"

She grins. "Yeah. Like the monkey jump."

"Right, because this is the natural way I would jump, hanging out between classes—barefoot, too, of course—while I wait around to be attacked."

"Be. More. Natural." She giggles.

"Be. More. Natural," I snort. I feel light-headed and have to sit down on the stairs.

"Are you okay?" Taylor says.

I take a few breaths and wave her off. "Too much sugar, I think. Thanks for stopping by," I say. "Happy Halloween."

"You, too. If you change your mind about the belt test, we're going out for pizza after. So you'd get free pizza out of it."

The thought of going to a belt test I'm not participating in makes my chest feel hollow.

After the door shuts behind her, I steel myself and walk into the kitchen. Hunter's replenishing the food and drinks, so I corner him and demand to know why he's hanging around tonight.

"I don't have any cash," he says.

"That's such a lie! You worked four nights at Dairy Dump this week."

"No cash," he repeats. "And don't call it that."

"Why not? It's what you have to take after you eat there."

"Shut up."

He pulls some bowls out of the cabinet so we can toss pretzels inside and make Chex Mix. It's so white of us. Ricky will be appalled.

"I think you want to get with Hannah," I say. "Because she's a challenge."

Hunter turns away, but I catch a flash of color on his face.

"Oh my God, I'm right, aren't I? Never gonna happen."

"Maybe I want to keep an eye on you and Rico Suave," he says.

I snort. "How? You're sitting in front of us."

Hunter regards me for a minute. "Have you kissed yet?"

I glance wildly toward the other room. "Shut up!"

He grins. "No? Why not?"

"Just 'cause *you* sleep with everyone the first chance you get . . ."

"I do not!"

"Doesn't mean I should."

"Who said anything about sleeping with him? You can kiss someone even if you're not soul mates. The world doesn't split in half."

Maybe. Maybe not. I think of Ricky and me in the garage gym last week, our endless mirror images surrounding us, and of one pair of us splitting off from the rest, creating an alternate universe.

Just then, Ricky pokes his head in. "Need any help?"

I immediately point to the pantry, praying he didn't hear any of my conversation with Hunter. "Sure. Can you grab the box of cereal, top shelf?"

He pulls it down. "Hexa Grains." He laughs. "What are these?"

"Generic for Chex."

"It sounds scary." He makes a spooky voice: "I put a hex on you."

"Or Penta-grahams: the satanic Teddy Grahams." We're laughing and lightly shoving each other, and I don't even see Hunter leave.

His words about kissing Ricky stay with me, though, like splinters under my skin.

17

AFTER DINNER ON MONDAY, HUNTER GIVES ME A SHEET OF postcard stamps and says I should give them to Shelly to make sure she keeps in touch. She and her mom are stopping by on their way to the airport. The naive collective known as our parents believes we've made up. Mom's rolling out the welcome mat by preparing popcorn and a vegetable platter. I wish Dad would eat the veggies plain instead of slathering them with ranch dressing.

"What if I don't want Shelly to keep in touch?" I ask Hunter, just to be contradictory.

He stuffs his face with popcorn. "I thought you guys were friends again."

"Sort of." I shrug. "I'm not sure." She hasn't been at school because she's been taking classes online, preparing to matriculate or whatever, and we haven't really talked since the time I went over to her house a couple of weeks ago.

"She can just e-mail," I say, flicking the stamps at Hunter. "You're so weird."

"Who wants e-mails from New York? It'd be like getting them from around the corner."

He has a point.

The doorbell rings and Hunter gets up from the table. "Do you want me to leave?"

"It's okay."

The last time Shelly was here, for my birthday, she and Hunter were all over each other, and she didn't even like him that way! They weren't in love; they weren't even dating.

He made me doubt my convictions yesterday, telling me kissing isn't a big deal, but of course that's what he'd say; he has no self-control. He doesn't know what it's like to hold out for something real, something meaningful.

Shelly barely acknowledges Hunter when she walks in, just gives him a quick smile and thanks him for the birthday card.

All of us sit down in the living room, but she only talks with me and my parents. Her mom and my mom get a bit emotional, remembering when we were "this tall"; Shelly and I look at each other and mimic them; my dad tells her about his favorite restaurant in New York, which happens to be near her new school, and she jots it down and promises to check it out.

"Oh, so here are these stamps, for postcards? If you want," I say. "No pressure, just—if you go somewhere cool and want to send a postcard, I'd love to know what you're up to."

She smiles. "Okay."

After her mom's car pulls away, Hunter and I head back into the kitchen.

"You're wigging me out," I tell him. "Why didn't you take credit for the stamps? Why are you being so nice?"

He grins. "You think I'm being nice?"

"Yes," I grumble.

"Cool. Maybe you could, you know, mention it to Hannah or something."

I'm immediately on guard. "Why?"

"I want Hannah to think I'm a good brother."

"Why don't you want *me* to think you're a good brother?"

"I want you to experience it and then tell Hannah."

I knew it. Hunter isn't nice. Hannah called him the worst brother ever, so he's out to prove her wrong. It's not about getting back on my good side at all.

"You can't stand it if one person doesn't like you," I say. "You need everyone to like you. It's pathological."

"And you don't care if no one likes you," he says.

"That's not true! And your reasons for being nice are faulty."

"No they're not. It's the same outcome. Look, I want to be a good brother. I know I haven't been, and she was right about that, but I'm different now. And if Hannah happens to find out about it, what's so bad about that?"

"She's the only friend I have left, that's what!" I yell. "Shelly's flying to New York; DJ hates me. You can't have Hannah."

"Okay, okay," he says, backing off. "Just . . . if you—"

"No."

"But if it should happen to come up—"

"No!"

"Love each other, children," comes Mom's dry voice from the living room.

It doesn't hit me until midnight that Shelly is gone. She hasn't just "flown to New York." My best friend is gone, and we never really cleared the air, and now we never will.

She'll never be at school with me again, and she'll never be a bike ride away. Even if she comes home next summer, it won't be the same. I squandered our last weeks together without realizing it, and then the diner happened and I only wanted to spend time with Ricky.

But he's temporary, too. He graduates next spring, just a few months away. What does it matter if we kiss or don't kiss? He'll be gone soon, just like everyone else.

I feel chilled, clammy. I'm alone. I can't go back to martial arts, I've lost my friends, I'm failing school—what's left? How am I supposed to spend the endless days ahead of me? I have nothing to work toward, nothing to achieve.

A poster hanging up at Shelly's ballet class said, "Life is short. Live for today," but what no one will ever tell you, what no adult will ever say, is that life is really very long.

All I want is to rest, but my imitation heart won't let me. I picture it beating in a worn-out husk of a scarecrow, all straw arms and legs, with buttons for eyes. I picture setting the scarecrow on fire, but even then I'd still exist, my heart thumping and twitching on the ground below.

Low.

Low to the ground is comforting; standing up is bad.

In my dream, I see the gunman's feet from under the table and I crawl out and sneak up on him from behind. I kick his legs out, and he falls onto his back. He's wearing a mask, just like in real life.

But then, when I try to punch him, I keep missing. Not a single one of my punches connects. They don't land anywhere near him. My fist hits the floor beside him, even though he's only a few centimeters away from me. I get desperate, panicky, but all my movements are slow and totally ineffective. Eventually he rolls to the side and picks up his gun and shoots me in the face.

When I burst awake, I have to bite my arm to keep from screaming.

I remember why I was covered in blood.

My face is damp, from tears or sweat—I'm not sure. I paw at my face, smear the wetness away.

It's almost pitch-black out, but I get dressed and leave the house. I walk in the direction of the train tracks, where Hunter and I used to play before Mom put a stop to it. I don't know why I'm going there except that I have to. I have to. I'll figure it out when I get there.

My feet carry me, but I don't feel the ground beneath me. It's like they're taking orders from someone else and I'm just along for the ride. That's how I felt when I yelled at DJ at school near my locker, and when I punched Ricky outside the principal's office. Like it wasn't me. Like I had no control over my actions.

It's after two, so the sidewalks are completely dark—almost no streetlights to guide me.

In the distance I hear a train passing through, the tail-end wheels screeching against the tracks. As I get closer, I see the red and white crossing arms flashing and lifting, and I think of school bus drivers having to open their doors and listen for the sounds of a train even when there's nothing there.

I know what I'm doing is crazy, but I can't stand the thought of going back to sleep and having more nightmares or, worse, lying there awake as the seconds tick by, reminding me that's all I have to look forward to: time passing.

I haven't gone wandering since the night Hunter followed me, and for a minute I swear I see a glimpse of Mom's Volvo. I duck into an alley and wait for the car to pass, and then I continue on my way.

The train station parking lot comes into view a few minutes later. It's tiny, home to a car with a bunch of broken windows, copper-colored rust scratches, and a flat-looking tire. Crushed beer cans, fast-food bags, and other garbage surround the abandoned car, implying there was a little party here recently. I nudge one of the beer cans over with my foot and watch cigarette butts fall out. I look inside the car and see a pipe, warped spoons, ripped-up seats, and burn marks.

I always wondered about abandoned cars. Where do they come from?

Do people *plan* where they're going to ditch the car, and, if so, how do they pick the spot? Do they bring a friend along for the ditching so they'll have a ride home after? Do they ever visit their old car, drive by and see if it's still there, condemned to an afterlife as a den for crackheads?

Maybe the car wasn't abandoned. Maybe this is where the car sputtered and died, right at this spot in the parking lot, and abandoned the *driver*. In which case, the car deserved to be left behind.

I was covered in blood because my arms and legs abandoned me. They betrayed me. They wouldn't do what I told them to do at the diner. They disobeyed me even though I screamed at them. They ignored me, and I can't trust them anymore.

I cry out and try to move faster, try to catch up with the train, but it's already passed the station, and I'm so tired that I end up dragging my legs like they don't belong to me, like nothing about my body belongs to me, which is true—but it's okay; it's better, actually, because if my body doesn't belong to me, it won't hurt to leave it behind.

I walk over to the tracks and look down at them. I turn around slowly so my traitorous feet don't get tangled up, and I take in my surroundings, the station and parking lot. I look in all directions, and then I sit down and let my legs dangle off the platform, right above the tracks. I think about the stories about kids on bicycles getting their wheels stuck on the tracks and not moving in time and what would happen if I sat here until the next train came, my legs dangling over the side—

"Imogen. Imogen!" Hunter flies toward me out of nowhere, like he teleported off a spaceship. So he *was* tracking me. *Again.* "Get in the car," he yells, pointing in the direction of the street. "Now."

I just stare at him.

He grabs me by the elbow. "What are you doing? Are you running away?!"

It's almost sweet that he thinks that. He sees a girl playing hoboes, not scheming to have her legs ripped off.

"The train already came by," I say, my words flat and plain and logical.

"Jesus, Imogen, you're really scaring me," he cries, shaking me by the shoulders and trying to make me look at him.

I refuse to meet his eyes. I go limp instead, let my knees buckle, because it's not my body anyway. He has to wrap his arm around my waist to keep me upright. He half pulls, half carries me, and we're just passing the abandoned car when Hunter stops, his face contorted, and he's about to speechify some more, when I see two squad cars pull up, lights flashing. The world spins and my eyes lose focus.

"Hey," sounds a male voice on the loudspeaker. "What are you kids doing?"

Two cops get out of the car; they're coming toward us—

"Get down!" I tackle Hunter's legs and slam him to the ground like a linebacker. He goes down with a thud, scraping his palms and face, and I cover him with my body.

"Don't shoot, don't shoot," I scream. "Don't hurt him, please don't hurt him, he's my brother, don't shoot, oh God, please don't shoot, don't shoot, please, *please* don't hurt my brother—"

Tears blur my vision until I don't have eyes anymore; I just have the endless rising tide of an ocean clogging my throat and lungs, pulling me under, but I keep holding on to Hunter, making sure no part of him is accessible. They'll have to go through me first; they can't hurt him, not him, not Hunter . . .

I kick and scream, no words anymore, just noises I didn't know I could make, sounds I didn't know I had in me.

It takes three cops to pull me off him.

18

I CROUCH ON THE LIVING ROOM FLOOR AT HOME, ROCKing back and forth, fists rubbing at my eyes, bluntly stabbing my cheeks, but the tears won't stop. Mom and Dad sit on the couch, clasping hands and trembling with concern while Hunter tries to console me from a distance. No one comes near me; they don't know what I'll do.

Officer Jenkins could have pressed charges against me—I walloped him pretty good—but he recognized me from the diner and told the other guys to take it easy on me.

"I know you feel like you failed the cashier," Hunter says quietly.

"I didn't fail the cashier. I failed *him*."

"Who? The gunman?"

"He wasn't gonna hurt her," I moan. "The cashier knew him. She goes, 'What the hell are you doing, Daryl?' And he could've shot her, but he didn't. He hit her with the gun, but he didn't shoot her."

"He knocked her teeth out; she had to have pretty complicated surgery on her jaw."

They were arguing, and he was waving the gun around, and she was crying when the cops showed up, with the flashing lights and the loudspeaker. They told Daryl to come out with his hands on his head, but he wouldn't do it. I could hear the feet of the cops, and I could see them at the windows and the doors on the opposite side from my corner under the table. I was flat on the ground and I could see it. They pointed their guns at him and told him to drop his weapon.

He was holding the gun at his side. *All he had to do was open his hand and let it go.* Just open his hand and let it go, but he wouldn't, and they crept closer.

Drop it, drop it.

But he wouldn't drop it.

Everyone was yelling at him . . .

Drop it, drop it.

Drop your weapon.

I can't think about this.

I can't say this out loud.

I don't want to see it in my head, ever again.

If we stop now, I won't have to see it.

"They told him to drop his weapon . . . ," I murmur, squeezing my eyes shut.

"Yes? And?" Hunter says.

"I had to do something. I had to do something, because he didn't know I was there . . ."

I crawled out from under the table and stood, like a baby bird unfolding from its egg.

Kick him, punch him, shove him from behind, I told myself, *or they're gonna kill him. Do it. Now! Do it!*

Half of my brain was screaming at me to act, and the other half was screaming *Gun*. My body decided on paralysis.

Daryl turned and looked at me, the yolky whites of his eyes peeking out from his ski mask, like long-dead stars in an endless black universe.

He lifted his gun and pointed it right at me . . .

I closed my eyes, felt a warm trickle of pee down my leg. I closed my eyes and prepared to die. My eyes were closed, but I heard the words.

Light him up.

I don't know if I'm talking or thinking.

"Is that what they said? 'Light him up'?" Mom is right by my ear. My eyes are still shut and I'm rocking and rocking on the carpet, but I feel her cool, smooth hand on my arm.

And then they ripped him apart with bullets, and the blood splattered my face and my clothes. So wet and warm, the blood, so much of it, all over me, matted and sticky, his body a crumpled sack of skin and bones that used to be a human being with parents and friends and dreams and hopes and even though he was stupid . . .

"He didn't need to die that way. He didn't need to die," I moan, pounding my fists into the carpet. "They killed him because of me."

"Imogen, listen to me," says Dad. "Sweetheart. It's not your fault."

Dad swims into focus, sitting on the couch, and then blurs away again as I wipe the water from my eyes.

"He wasn't going to hurt her. Stupid, stupid, stupid . . ." I bash my cheek with the side of my fist and I don't even feel it.

Feel it. Feel it. Feel something.

I'm not mad at myself for not attacking a man with a gun. I'm mad I didn't prevent the cops from attacking *him*. I'm supposed to prevent unnecessary fights. To defend the weak. It was three against one. He was the weak one. He was the weak one.

"He wasn't gonna shoot her," I repeat.

"But you don't know that for sure—"

"Why did she know his name, then? Why did she call him Daryl? Maybe they planned it together, and then she changed her mind. If I'd just been brave, I could have kicked his legs out, prevented the whole thing. But I froze up, and they killed him."

"He pointed a gun at you!"

I should've stayed under the table. I was scared they were going to kill him, and then I made it so they *had* to kill him. Stupid fucking idiot.

"He was waving the gun at everyone, not just you. They didn't have a choice," Hunter insists.

"But if I'd done something before they arrived . . ." I melt into the carpet, sobbing and clutching it. "I would've won! Do you understand that? He didn't know I was there."

Mom and Dad try to get me to go upstairs and get into bed, but I can't get up. The floor wants me, and I feel safe here, low to the ground, hidden.

It's much better than my room, which is empty and lifeless.

Every day it reminds me I'm not who I thought I was; my identity is as blank as the walls.

I wish I were five years old and Dad were strong again, so he could carry me up anyway and tuck me in.

I stay on the floor, and Mom covers me with blankets and positions a pillow softly under my head.

19

HUNTER'S GOT A BANDAGE ON HIS CHEEK FROM WHERE I slammed him to the ground, and he picks at it obsessively, peeling and resealing the tape, as he drives me to school a day later.

There goes that male-modeling career, I think, because if I don't, I'll have to wonder, how can he stand it? How can he stand having a coward for a sister?

Ricky waits for me outside Mrs. H.'s at the usual time.

"Ready to go in?" he asks.

"Does she know you're out here?"

"Not yet. She's on the phone."

"Come with me." I tug on his sleeve, lead him around the corner.

"What's up?" he says, placing his hand against the wall above my head. "Are you okay?"

"I remembered some things a couple nights ago."

"Is that why you weren't here yesterday?"

I nod. "It was bad."

He moves to block me off from the rest of the hallway, protecting me from any scrutiny. Leans down and asks softly, "How bad?"

Walking around the train tracks in the middle of the night bad. Scaring the hell out of my family bad.

"Hold my hand for a moment?" I ask.

"As long as you want."

We stand there silently. I feel my fake heart rate slow down. If I were hooked up to a monitor, I'm certain it would prove the effect he has on me, how my entire being relaxes.

"Should we go in?" Ricky says after a minute.

I take a deep breath. "Yeah."

"Let's pretend we're in couples counseling." He smiles at me, testing the waters. I smile back.

"He never asks for directions."

"Nag, nag, nag."

Ricky squeezes my hand and we round the corner. I'm sad

when he lets go, but we can't let Mrs. H. see us that way. She probably wouldn't approve.

"What made you choose Tae Kwon Do?" Mrs. Hamilton asks. "What drew you to it?"

"Hunter and I enrolled at the same time, but he dropped out because he got bored practicing by himself. He likes team sports better. When he left, I realized it was my best chance to outshine him at something. I had to get so amazing, so fast, that he would never want to return."

"So you did it because you wanted to be better than Hunter at something?"

"No, I wanted to learn how to take care of myself. I liked the idea of having honor, of behaving a certain way no matter what, of following the Children's Home Rules."

Bad answer, because now she has a homework assignment for me. As if I don't have enough going on in my regular classes.

"Is there any reason you can't still live your life according to those precepts?" she wonders.

"What precepts?"

"The Children's Home Rules."

I snort. "Those are for third graders."

"So they don't apply to you anymore?"

"That's not what I mean."

"Is there any reason you can't live your life that way?"

"Other than the fact that it's lame?" I say.

She waits.

"I guess not," I mutter.

"I want you to find your old sheet of Children's Home Rules and follow them for the next month and see how you feel."

I roll my eyes. "Does Ricky have to follow them, too?"

"Ricky has a different assignment."

But neither of them will tell me what it is.

"Greetings, Mother!" I say sarcastically when I walk through the front door. "Greetings, Father!"

No one responds.

This is beyond stupid.

"Greetings, family," I scream.

"What are you doing?" calls Hunter from upstairs.

"Children's Home Rule number one: Children will greet their parents when they come home, and say good-bye to them when they leave."

"Oh my God, are you like, reverting?"

"Greetings, Brother."

A pause.

"Greetings, Sister."

The next morning I wake up with a fever and a stuffy nose. It's a relief. If I'm sick, I can stay in bed. I don't have to pretend to pay attention in class. I can fall even further behind without being blamed for it. I can rest.

I wish Mom would sit in my desk chair by the bed and read to me. Even *Bleak House* would be okay; maybe if someone else read it to me I'd understand it better. But she just sort of laughs when I suggest this and reheats some Campbell's in a can. I feel lonely on the second floor by myself all day. The intercom connects us, but it's not the same.

Ricky comes over after school with tortilla soup: his grandmother's. It's the best soup I've ever had. I never want to touch the canned stuff again.

By Sunday, I've pretty much kicked my cold, so Ricky shows up again and we practice for a while in the garage. We're working on elbow slams and sidekicks.

It's our longest workout yet. An hour in, I offer to get us water from the house, and when I return he's standing against the wall, his back to the mirror, still breathing hard. I know it's from exercising, but it feels . . . sexy to see him that way, his chest expanding and deflating as he looks over and smiles at me.

He wipes the sweat off his brow with the bottom of his T-shirt, and I catch a sweet little glimpse of his stomach, the line of skin between his shirt and his boxers.

The line of skin is the perfect shape to trace with my finger. My nonheart flips double-time at this thought.

I hand him his bottle of water, and our fingers touch. We're close enough that I can feel the warmth pouring off his skin. His sweat smells clean, like bread, and I love that our bodies are the same level of damp and warm.

"You gonna let go of that?" he teases, and I blush, releasing the bottle and his hand.

We chug our waters like it's a contest, and I watch his Adam's apple bobbing in his throat, and I want, more than anything, to know what he tastes like there, and not just there but on the side of his neck, right where it meets his shoulder, and I'm looking at his mouth, his perfect, full lips, and wondering what it would be like to stop *thinking* about this and *do* something about it, to fall into good emotions instead of bad ones, and he must be wondering the same thing because he takes my hands in his, making me spill and drop my water bottle, and he pulls me in and we're doing just that—kissing, hard, our mouths coming together and apart.

We alternate top and bottom lips; we can't decide which way to kiss because they're both so good and there's so much we want to do, and the air vibrates between us, the places we're not touching. Every second slows down until all I feel is the pulse in my neck quivering like hummingbird wings, so fast I need to gasp.

He waits till I'm practically begging before gliding his tongue against mine. The cold water chilling both our tongues makes a delicious contrast to the heat of our skin.

We keep kissing, and I wrap my arms tightly around his neck. I glance in the mirror at the hundreds of other Imogens who do the same.

And then I close my eyes.

Ricky left two hours ago, but I'm still high from our kiss. I run my tongue over my lips, which feel puffy, like shiny balloons.

I fantasize about calling Shelly, but I call Hannah instead.

She squeals when I tell her what happened. Then she says, "Hang on, what's that noise I hear in the distance?"

"What noise?"

"Oh, just the peal of wedding bells. Can't you hear it?"

"What? No! I'm just hoping he couldn't tell that was my first kiss."

Hannah channels her inner DJ and goes into lecture mode. "If you'd gone for it on our triple date this summer, you wouldn't be worried. You'd already have a kissing session under your belt."

"I wasn't going to use someone for practice," I protest.

"We don't all meet our future husbands the first time out.

Sometimes you can just have fun; it doesn't always have to mean something."

"I want it to mean something, or why do it?"

"Okay, it should mean something," she relents, "but it doesn't have to mean *everything*."

"You realize who you sound like right now, don't you?" I grumble.

"Who?"

"My dumbass brother."

"I take it all back," she laughs. "This conversation never happened. So. Tell me what you like best about Ricky."

"It's not his looks, even though he's really hot. It's more like a feeling." I think of his eyes, the flecks of gold like a lantern leading me through the dark. I think of sunsets and roasting marshmallows around a fire, the longing I felt as a kid on camping trips, wishing the night would never have to end.

20

RICKY AND I SHOW UP TO COUNSELING WITH KLEENEX boxes in tow.

"You're both sick?" Mrs. Hamilton says.

"Isn't it a nutty coincidence?" I say, looking right at Ricky, dabbing my lips slowly with a tissue and daring him to hold my gaze. "Can you even believe it? What are the odds?"

Ricky's eyes blow up like puffer fishes and his foot jumps, tapping loudly on the floor.

Mrs. Hamilton turns to him. "Something to add?"

"If she finds out, there's no way she'll let us continue," Ricky chastises me after counseling.

"Okay, you're right. I'm sorry. I won't joke around anymore. But you should've seen your face." I giggle.

"I was scared you were gonna lick your lips like Catwoman or something."

"Are we working out today?"

He shakes his head. "I can't even breathe."

"I'm so sorry for getting you sick."

He straightens up, affects a mock military voice. "I knew the risks. I volunteered for the mission."

"Does your grandma have any of that amazing soup left?"

"Come over after school and find out."

I haven't been to Ricky's place since our date. I'd rather spend the afternoon working out in the garage, but I can't exactly force him to exercise when he's fighting off the very cold I gave to him.

For the first twenty minutes after we arrive, Ricky does chores. He collects the garbage and recycling and sets them out on the street for pickup tomorrow. Then he sweeps the kitchen floor. I offer to help because it seems weird sitting at the table drinking a ginger ale while he works, but he tells me he's almost done, and then he takes my hand and leads me to the living room.

The TV's behind a closed cabinet in the corner instead of the main focal point of the room, like at my house.

It doesn't take long before sitting on his living room floor doing homework turns into lying sideways on his living room floor and making out. I bring my leg up over his hip and he gently stops me.

"Slow down a bit," he whispers, between kisses.

"Sorry," I say, embarrassed, retreating. The only time I can forget my life is when we're fooling around. It feels nice to fall into oblivion.

He kisses me again, just a quick one. "Nothing to be sorry about. It's just, we both have enough going on; I don't want you to have to deal with that stress."

"What stress?"

"Of having sex."

I didn't think we were anywhere near having sex, but Ricky looks so worried and concerned about me that I don't push it.

"Did you go that far with your ex-girlfriend?" I ask.

"Yeah, but we were both seventeen."

"So you've done it before."

"Just a couple of times."

I look away. "I don't want to know."

"The third time—"

Three isn't a couple. Three is a few. Three is *three*.

"The third time, the condom broke and we had to get the morning-after pill and it was a whole nightmare. We blamed each other and nothing was the same after that. I don't want that for us."

"Was it worth it?"

"No, that's what I'm trying to tell you. It's not worth it. Not right now . . ." He's getting upset. "I want you to feel totally safe with me. I don't want there to be anything weird between us. Ever."

"Ricky," I say, tears in my eyes, "the *only* time I feel okay is when I'm with you. I don't have anything else. I'm sorry if that scares you. My family's messed up; school's messed up. You're the only place."

"I know—for me, too. I can't screw this up."

He kisses my tears away, and I run my fingers through his soft, thick hair while he closes his eyes and nuzzles my neck. "I wish I could forget all about the diner," he says. "Just a blank sheet covering up those memories."

I close my eyes and sink into him. "I wish you hadn't been there, but thank you for being there, thank you."

He presses kisses along my cheek and ear and nose and mouth. "It'll be all right," he tells me.

Anyone else would be lying. When Ricky says it, I believe him.

When it's time for me to go, I feel restless, unproductive. I haven't gotten the kind of endorphin rush I'm used to getting with Ricky. Kissing was great, but without martial arts or some kind of workout, I'm on edge.

My original plan was to teach him how to fight me for real. How long do I have to wait?

Ricky offers to drive me home, but I'd rather walk. I have all this unspent energy coiled up inside me, so I call home and tell them I'll be a bit late.

I walk past boarded-up stores and security grates pulled down and a few low-rent bars with the names of beer brands lit up in neon in the windows. The cars that were there the first time I came to Ricky's with my apology cookies are still there, seemingly in the exact same locations, with the exact same flyers jammed behind their windshield wipers. The only difference is now they're slick with melting snow, proving that the seasons have changed and the world's gone by all around them.

Flyers are stapled to wooden telephone poles, too, with tear-off phone numbers dangling down, advertising the same things from September: "Accent Elimination," "Work from Home" scams, and "Ladies Only!" events.

"Ladies Only!" for what? I wonder this time. There's no mention of a particular bar. I tear it off the pole for a closer look and realize with a start it's been waiting for me to notice it for months. It's been waiting for me this whole time to come back and find it.

Amateur Fight Nights!

Ladies Only!

Must be 18!

$100 cash

www.me-owfightnights.com

After dinner I lock my bedroom door, boot up my computer, and type in the (admittedly bizarre) Web site address. An embedded, low-res video starts up the second I enter the site. I fumble to turn the volume down.

The camera work is all over the place, trying to look gritty and real. Six female fighters pose awkwardly onstage at some underground bar. Men on all sides of the ring surround them.

The women look like reanimated dead strippers: caked-on makeup, ridiculously long nails, high heels and push-up bras, barely-there miniskirts and visible thong straps.

The Web site promoter looks like Matthew McConaughey's shorter, evil twin; he speaks with a drawling southern accent.

"Before you begin, state your name and age for the camera," he says. He joins the contenders onstage and holds a microphone right up to their lips.

"I'm Mercedes and I'm nineteen," says one with a Minnie Mouse voice. Her skin is rough-looking and her eyes are black and soulless, like flies crawling around a pile of dog shit. (If she's nineteen, I'm prenatal.)

"I'm Peaches and I'm twenty," says the other. Maaaaaybe.

“Welcome to Kitty Kat Fights,” says the promoter. “Where scratching, hair pulling, and straddling is not just encouraged, it’s required, ladies. Meow-ow-ow.”

Oh, kill me now.

The male audience cheers. I want to stop watching, but I can’t. I want to see them fight.

“Each bout is ten rounds, each round is ninety seconds; last girl standing per fight makes a hundred bucks cold, hard cash.”

The camera pans over to a girl wearing sweatpants, sneakers, and a T-shirt. I lean forward in my chair. That’s more like it. That’s what *I* would’ve worn.

“What do you think of her outfit?” the promoter asks, holding his microphone out to the audience.

The men are not pleased. “Booo!”

“Is this your first time here, honey?”

She nods coquettishly and bites one of her fingers.

He chuckles and addresses the crowd again. “We have a virgin!”

Cheers and leers from the men.

“Okay, let me tell you how this works, sweetheart. You gotta ditch that ponytail, fluff your hair, roll down the top of your pants so we can get a peek at your panties, and tie that shirt in a knot above your belly button. We’re looking for sexy kittens, not dykes. And ice those nipples for the boys at home.”

Ewww!

"Don't come back until you learn how to dress." The men verbally assault her off the stage.

Furious, the designated tomboy pushes "Mercedes" on her way offstage. Mercedes pushes back. They take a couple wild swings at each other—awful form, no training whatsoever—and then fall on the floor and start rolling around. The camera circles them and then zooms in for a close-up as they lean in to kiss each other! Just as their lips touch, the image cuts off abruptly and a new link appears, directing me to a paying site to finish watching.

I shut the computer off, incensed.

I knew it was dumb the second I saw their clothes. I should've closed out of the screen as soon as the video started. *Of course* it was sex related. The only way female fighters could possibly interest anyone is if there's a chance they'll rip each other's clothes off. Nobody will just let us fight.

I want to hurl my computer monitor to the floor, but I don't want to draw attention to myself or have to explain what I was doing at that site. With each breath tearing through my lungs, my pretend heart shrinks, crushed by a vise into something even harder and more compact than it already is.

I go downstairs and spend twenty minutes beating the hell out of the punching bag in the garage. I picture Daryl in his ski mask, eyes hollow and empty. I picture the cops storming the place. I picture the stupid women in the videos, and I picture guys at home in their rooms watching the videos online, drooling over the images and reaching for their credit cards with sweaty hands.

I fight them all in my head, over and over, but it doesn't make a dent in my frustration. Not even close.

21

AT SCHOOL THE NEXT DAY I FEEL CALMER, MOSTLY BEcause I'll be seeing Ricky. It's enough to know he's somewhere in the school, going through the motions, hearing the same bells and announcements, keeping my heart safe for me. I'd like to return the favor, but I don't think his is in my chest. The ticktocking thing I've been carting around isn't human; it's not even a heart. Sometimes I think it's a bomb.

Ricky should be over his/our cold soon and up for a real sparring session, no holding back. I need it now more than ever.

Right before counseling, we take a private moment in the hallway again. He makes sure we're far enough around the corner from Mrs. Hamilton's office that there's no way she can see us, and then he kisses me hello.

"Hey, cutie." His voice sends a delicious feeling through my body, like pouring warm apple cider down my throat and feeling it spread through my limbs.

"What're you doing for Thanksgiving?" I ask.

"My mom's giving a speech or something at the parade, and my dad and sister are gonna be home, so that's cool."

"Very cool. Your dad's on leave?"

"Yeah."

I'm happy for him but sad for me—guess we won't be hanging out.

"I'm not really into football, though, so I could sneak out after we eat on Thursday."

"Yay." We kiss.

"What about you? Gobble gobble?" He pretends to devour my neck.

"My mom's taking Hunter to look at colleges in DC, so it's probably pizza this year."

Mom and Hunter's flight is at 6:00 a.m. on Thanksgiving Day. They got a ridiculously cheap deal. After my attempt to "run away," which is still what they think I was doing, Mom offered to cancel the trip, but I can't handle any additional guilt, so I told them to go.

I have a nightmare around four, right as they're preparing to leave for O'Hare.

I dream I'm under the table at the diner, nothing new, but when I stand up and look out the windows, I see the paramedics trying to revive a bloody gunshot victim. They charge the defibrillator, three times, four times, and that's when I realize it's me. I watch my own blue-tinted corpse get zipped into a body bag and taken away on a stretcher.

When I wake, Hunter's by my side, holding my clammy hand in his firm, dry one.

"Same one as last time?" he asks.

I shake my head.

"Do you want us to stay?" he says. "Seriously." He looks almost as pale and haggard as I do. I want to tell him, "Yes, stay. I can't sleep if you're not in the next room, because who will help me? Who will take care of me?"

"No, you should go; it's okay. I'll be fine," I insist.

"I don't even want to go." He rubs his face and swipes tense fingers through his hair. He looks miserable, which surprises me and gives me something besides my dream to focus on.

"Why not? Don't you want to see Mom's old school?" She was magna cum laude at Georgetown University in the eighties, majoring in art history. Which kind of begs the question, What is she doing as a concierge at a hotel?

"I'm sure it's a good school, but . . ." Hunter's shoulders lift and fall, like a pile of dead leaves kicked up by the wind and resettling, flatter than before.

"She's kind of obsessed with you going there," I mention.

"Her friend is like head of alumni relations; she scored us a meeting with the dean, and a great hotel deal, and a tour with a guy who's going to be interning at the White House, and I should be excited, but . . ."

"Two buts in a row."

"I'm just not sure about going away for college. I know I should want to, but I'm just not sure."

"You're so good at school, though."

"That's 'cause I like school." He smiles sadly. "Don't make that face. I like seeing my friends all day and learning and being on teams, you know?"

"You could get in anywhere," I tell him.

"I know I could get in *somewhere*. It's the 'anywhere' that bothers me."

Mom comes up the stairs and pokes her head in my room. "Imogen, why are you up?" she asks, standing in my doorway. "Hunter, are you all packed? Time to go."

"She had a nightmare," he says, annoyed.

"Oh, dear. Are you okay?" Mom walks in and smooths the hair back from my forehead. I dodge her hand, pissed that she wants to help now, right when she's leaving. She lives downstairs, like a landlord. She doesn't get to help right now.

"It's nothing. Have a safe trip. Have fun," I say, and Hunter gives me a sympathetic look behind her back.

"We'll call when we get there. Dad's ordered a great meal for Thanksgiving, all the works, and hey—no cleanup."

I force a smile. She smiles back, looking strained around the eyes.

Children's Home Rule number two: Children will keep their rooms organized and clean.

Easy. There's nothing *in* my room.

I lug the vacuum upstairs and go over the carpeting three times, until the stripes all line up in perfect rows. I throw my sheets in the washer and fluff my pillows. I dust my shelves and nightstand.

Cleaning used to feel satisfying. I liked knowing I'd be sleeping in a soft, cottony bed, liked knowing it was clean because I'd put effort into it instead of waiting for Mom to do it.

Now I don't register anything I'm doing. I move like an automaton. Cleaning's just another way to kill time, so I won't have to go downstairs.

Dad and I eat in front of the TV, passing around containers of turkey slices and buttered rolls. We watch four different football games. Because of his job writing about sports, we get stations like ESPN Full Court and ESPN Game Plan and all the sports packages. If we plan it right, we won't have to exchange more than two words the entire holiday weekend.

I think about us sitting there, like father like daughter, both of us fake. Me with my fake heart, him with his wrong life. Did he wake up one morning missing something, the way I did? Can he even tell? Does he realize what we're lacking?

When the doorbell rings, I'm up like a shot.

"Expecting someone?" Dad sounds hurt and surprised, like our spectacular family-bonding meal has been interrupted.

"Just Ricky. We'll be in the garage, okay?"

"You can work out on a full stomach?"

"We'll warm up first," I say and open the front door.

But Ricky of course has to be polite and insists on going in the living room and saying hi to my dad.

(Children's Home Rule number 1: Children will greet their parents when they enter the home, and say good-bye to them when they leave.)

They chatter inanely for ten minutes, and it hits me.

The reason Ricky doesn't have to follow the Children's Home Rules is because he already does, and Mrs. Hamilton knows it. Ricky is actually respectful to everyone; he's the version of me I was only playing at all these years.

When his grandmother tells him to do something, he does it. He takes his shoes to the rummage sale, and he buys them back later. He takes out the garbage for his mother. He cleans the kitchen and he cleans his room because those are things you do, as part of a family, when no one's watching; you don't do them half-assed and then brag about them just to earn your next belt color.

I think of Grandmaster Huan telling the beginner belts, "Martial Arts is a code. Martial Arts is a way of life, not to be picked up and dropped when it's convenient."

"Ricky *hates* football," I announce at last.

"Oh," says Dad, picking up the remote. "Sorry. We can change it."

"That's okay," says Ricky, giving me a hard look. It pisses me off that he's so respectful to my dad and I'm not, that he's more of a martial artist than I am, and how with this one look he's called me on it.

A half hour later we finally escape to the garage, and Ricky sets his gym bag down and reaches for my hand.

"Hey," he says, drawing me in for a kiss. "Happy Thanksgiving."

I'm still annoyed so I break it off.

He's surprised. "What's wrong?"

"Let's fight," I say, bouncing lightly back and forth on the balls of my feet. Between the diner, that pathetic Kitty Kat fight club, and the fact that I haven't been to class in months, I'm itching for a beat-down. His or mine, it doesn't really matter. "Try to punch me in the face."

Ricky laughs.

That nervous habit of his has got to go.

"Come on," I say, waving him near. "Just try."

"Right now?"

"Well, what did you think we were training for? I want to know what it's like to be in a real fight." My adrenaline, always rushing beneath the surface, dictates my words.

"Right. Ricky Ricardo punches the helpless little white girl. And then my mom's out of the election."

"I won't tell anyone how it happened. I'll say I got jumped downtown. And that's assuming you'll even land a punch."

"I'm twice your size and weight," he scoffs. "I could pick you up and haul you over my shoulder right now."

"So try it, then! I've already punched you. I know what I'm doing."

"Yeah, when I wasn't expecting it," he snaps.

I remember the fortune cookie he made up on our date: "You'll be sucker punched in the face by a really cute girl."

He doesn't count my punch. He was impressed it hurt so much, but he doesn't count it. It was a sucker punch, not a real punch. I cheated. That's what he thinks. That I'm "cute." An adorable spitfire he can use to learn how to fight. An ineffective little girl who's kidding herself and has been for years.

"You won't fight me for real? You think you have to hold back?" I say, incredulous.

He won't look at me. "I don't want to hurt you."

"You don't think *I* could hurt *you*?"

"This is stupid."

"It's not stupid to me! Just—come on, let's go." I step forward and shove his chest with both my hands. He steps back with one foot to right himself but doesn't lift his hands. "Oh my God, you're fucking kidding me. Let's go!"

"I'm not punching you in the face."

"You won't be able to! That's my point! Just try. I'll block it, I'll dodge it, I'll counterattack. I just want a real fight. To show what I can do."

"I don't want to punch my girlfriend, okay?" he cries.

"Oh my God." I realize. "This is because we kissed, isn't it?"

"No, of course not."

"It is! I knew we shouldn't have gone there," I say. "What we had was better; it was more important, and now it's ruined."

"It has nothing to do with that. Even if we'd never kissed, I'd be saying the same thing."

"You didn't mind punching me in the arm," I point out. "That first week of lessons."

"You tricked me into doing that!"

"How did I trick you? That doesn't even make sense."

We look at each other, chests heaving, but this time I don't think it's sexy. This time I don't want to touch him except to hit him, or to get him to hit me.

"You have some weird ideas about relationships," he says.

"So now I'm weird, too. Great."

"That's not what I meant." He sighs. "Can we drop it?"

I'm begging now, shifting my weight from foot to foot, holding my fists up like we're about to spar any second. "Try me. Just let me try."

"I'm gonna go," he says after a long pause. "Call me if you ever calm down."

"Don't talk to me like that."

He chuckles angrily and shakes his head. "Oh man, I should have known when you punched me in the hallway. I should've known you were a nutcase."

"And you're a condescending asshole."

If a girl punches someone, she's crazy. If a guy punches someone, he's dealing with his feelings. He's normal.

"Leave if you're gonna leave," I shout.

I kick the punching bag so hard the chains rattle and threaten to fall off their hinges.

After he yanks the door shut behind him, there's another long pause and then his car horn blares for, like, thirty seconds straight, followed by a series of sporadic blares. I think he's slamming his hand on the horn, open-palmed.

I fling the door open and race outside, hoping to catch up with him, but when I get to the street, his car's gone.

Dizzy, dazed, and out of it, I stumble back inside the garage gym. My body and brain and voice are hostile strangers; they're still not my own.

If I hadn't given in to feeling good with him before, if I hadn't let myself feel comfort and pleasure in his arms, I'd be getting what I wanted right now. *Stupid Imogen, you wrecked your one chance for a fight. You had to be a girlie girl, and now that's all he sees you as.*

I want to punch myself in the face, bust open my lip, teach it to know better. Screw kissing and gentle caresses. That's not what I need right now.

I stare at my face in the mirror and I start punching. I punch until I shatter the glass, and then I punch until I hit the concrete behind it. I punch and punch and punch, and I cry out, but there's no pain, just shock and elation and the sound of fist hitting wall, thunk-thunk-thunk, because that's what I told my hand to do, and it's goddamn going to do WHAT I TELL IT TO DO, until I stop for a split second and see that the limb that used to be my hand is a shredded mess of pulp and flapping skin and glass, a bloody, smashed apricot impaled on exposed bone.

And then I start to scream.

22

WHEN WE GET BACK FROM THE ER, I'M FLOATING LIKE A buoy on a vast, empty sea of painkillers, too far away from shore to register what I've done. It feels like it happened to someone else's hand and that I'll wake up any second and my skin and bones will be restored.

But when I really look, I see it isn't true. I have to wear a plaster splint until my follow-up appointment in a month. Doctors actually have a term for this kind of break: a *brawler's fracture*. They knew immediately how it happened. I had to get stitches and a tetanus shot, too.

Not the Thanksgiving my dad was expecting.

He cried when the doctor brought me out. "I don't know how to help you. Tell me how to help you," he said.

"Be the way you used to be," I slurred.

I manage to clean up our takeout feast with just my left hand, cramming the paper boxes clumsily into the trash while Dad makes a choked phone call to Mom in DC.

She doesn't ask to speak to me. Maybe she thinks I'm asleep.

Strangely, I feel better about my chances for sleep tonight: (a) my room's superclean and (b) I've done something to make amends. I've marked what happened at the diner on my body now; it doesn't just exist in my head as a guilty memory. It's real, and it has a form and a shape, so maybe God or whoever will see I'm sorry and I won't have nightmares anymore.

"Do you want to sleep down here again?" Dad says when I'm halfway up the stairs. "Not the floor—we can make up the couch. That way I'm close by if you need me for anything."

"No, I'm okay. I want my own bed. Thanks, though."

"I'd like to hold on to those pills for you," he says carefully, opening his hand.

"Why?"

"I just think it would be better if I hold on to them. I'll give you one every few hours."

"I'm not gonna kill myself," I scoff.

"I'd like to hold on to them."

"Oh my God, I'm not gonna swallow them."

"Imogen, give me the pills."

"Maybe I should be worried about *you* taking them."

He gapes at me. "What?"

"Here." I dart down the stairs and veer off to the bathroom before he can stop me (like he could stop me), wrench open the child-safety lid, and pour the pills into the toilet. "Happy now?"

I flush.

"Why did you do that?" he asks sadly once I emerge from the bathroom. "You're going to be in a lot of pain."

Doesn't he know by now that I don't want anyone to save me—I want to suffer. If I'm dead, that defeats the purpose. This is not a cry for help: it's a means unto itself.

I fall asleep, no dreams, just as I'd hoped: total blankness. But then I wake up a few hours later with my hand on fire, throbbing like it's got its own heart. It steals the circulation from the rest of my body, until I don't have a body; I only have a hand. It's the rest of me that needs to be removed.

I bite my other fist and moan as tears pour down my face.

A couple of minutes go by, and the intercom next to my head crackles to life.

"Are you okay?" Dad says, his words a soft, momentary balm.

"It hurts," I gasp.

"Come down here and get some Tylenol," he says. "Come downstairs."

"I don't want to get out of bed."

"I can't bring anything to you up there."

"I know."

This is the way it should be. Daryl died because of me. It's right that I should feel pain.

A long pause from the intercom, but he's got the button secured somehow, maybe pressed down by a mug or a book, because I hear rustling and then a moment later I hear the plucking of guitar strings. A simple melody starts up, one of his favorite Beatles songs, about a blackbird who's broken and needs to learn how to fly.

Dad's voice emerges, trembling and unsure, but growing stronger with each line.

23

DAD SANG FOR AN HOUR, GOING THROUGH HIS OLD REPertoire: some Simon and Garfunkel, another Beatles, a couple of lullabies, and I know this sounds impossible, but while he was singing, I was transported. I closed my eyes, and I could pretend I was ten years old again, and none of this had ever happened, and nothing else bad would ever happen to me again.

In the morning I accept an over-the-counter pill with breakfast. I kind of miss the prescription stuff from last night, but the floaty feeling hadn't seemed fair; it took away too much, and I'm determined to feel as much of my hand's pain as possible without passing out or being unable to function.

Homework's out of the question, since I can't write, but

then Dad offers to type if I dictate. We sit down in front of the computer together like we're playing a duet.

A few hours later I'm dying to check my e-mail, so I make Dad turn his back while I slowly type in my password with my left hand.

There's a message from Ricky, with no subject line. I stop breathing.

I don't want to read it in Dad's office, so I print it, not allowing my eyes to focus on any of the words. It's a long one, and I'm scared of what it says. I tell Dad I need to go lie down, and I take the printout with me upstairs.

Hey Imogen,

I know I said all the wrong things yesterday and I'm sorry. I'm writing this in the middle of the night because I can't sleep. Having my dad home for Thanksgiving is fucked up. He criticizes almost everything I do, so when I come to your place and your dad is so nice, I don't understand why you don't see it. But I'm not writing to talk about my dad.

The truth is I'm still kind of mad about the punch. This is probably sexist but it really pissed me off you got the jump on me like that. But at the same time I was impressed; I couldn't stop thinking about it, and that's why I wanted to learn from you. You're really good at martial arts and you're also a seriously badass teacher. I work on my sidekicks every night in the yard, pivoting so it's almost a backward kick, where I look over my shoulder, just like you said.

The other reason I was mad about the punch that day in school was because I couldn't fight back, because then it would look like I was wailing on someone half my size. So when you gave me a chance to get even yesterday, I should've been happy, but I wasn't. First of all I never want to hurt you, but also, and this was what I couldn't say, I didn't want you to win again. Especially with my dad here.

It hurt that you called me an asshole because all I want to do is keep you safe. I know you don't need me to, and I know this will probably make you even angrier, but it's the truth. How can we get past this?

Ricky

I hunt and peck a reply: "Can't type, hurt my hand," but I don't click Send. He'll just call or text, all worried, and I don't want to explain things to him right now or make him feel like he has to come over again, when really he should be spending time with his dad, even if his dad's a jerk.

I don't get much more homework done over break, except for statistics. It's the only class I have that doesn't drive me crazy, because it has verifiable right or wrong answers. It's not open to interpretation.

Dad asks about continuing my homework but doesn't push too hard. We watch TV and comment on the insanity of the Christmas ads. Before I know it, it's Sunday night and the Volvo is pulling into the driveway, carrying Mom and Hunter back home.

I catch the tail end of their conversation as they tromp through the front hall, dropping their suitcases on the floor and hanging up their coats.

"If you still feel this way in six months, we'll talk about it again," Mom is saying.

That's her fallback position on everything.

I get up to greet them, in time to hear Mom's closing argument: "In the meantime, I think you should apply. What could it hurt?"

Hunter's glum expression tells me it could hurt a lot. He fixes his features when he sees me, though—sunny-side up with a slice of bacon. For a second I think Mom is going to hug me, but she just clears her throat and takes off her hat.

"Let's see that hand," she says, and I show her. She blinks a lot and grimaces, like I'm a house cat showing her a rancid squirrel I found.

"What happened?" Hunter asks.

"The mirror fell on my hand," I say.

"Repeatedly?" says Mom. Her voice cuts me. "Your father said you punched it."

I'm completely uncomfortable with how that image must look to her. She'll never understand why I did it, so it's pointless to explain. "It's over now. It'll be okay."

"You're lucky I have such good insurance," Mom says, passing by me on her way into the living room, pausing to drop a single kiss on my forehead, like a dirty penny falling into a well. What she doesn't know is that the penny will never reach bottom, because there is no bottom; I am endless in my need for her and whatever she's wishing about me will not be granted.

"Babe, we're home," she calls to Dad.

Her rapid blinking's been transferred to me, and as I'm doing it, I realize it's to prevent tears from forming.

"How'd it go?" I ask Hunter.

"Tell me you won't do it again," he says tiredly, placing a hand on my shoulder.

"I won't do it again," I promise.

Monday morning I let Hunter drive me to school, so no one will suspect me of ditching, and then right before the bell rings I walk back out and down the school steps, a quarter mile over to the train station.

Children's Home Rule number three: Children will respect their parents and teachers.

I want to respect Mom, but how can you respect someone you know nothing about?

I ride the train to Chicago and spy on her all day. She leaves the Congress Plaza Hotel early for lunch and walks through Grant Park to the Art Institute. She doesn't go to the Seurat exhibit, the *Sundays in the Park with George* one, like everyone else does; she goes straight for the Monet water lilies. It's the happiest and most peaceful I've seen her in months.

At home after dinner, I'm clearing the table when I drop a dirty dish on the floor, shattering it into pieces. I crouch to collect them and Mom cries, "Just leave it!" I look over at her and wonder if she basically hates me now.

Dad tells us to get out of Mom's hair so she can tidy up. Hunter's got a shift at Dairy Dump anyway, and on his way out the door he teases me: "This was all part of your plan, wasn't it? To get out of washing the dishes?"

Dad gets a wooden bowl of nuts and the nutcracker and takes them to the living room. I follow. Our nutcracker isn't one of those creepy soldier kinds with a face and teeth and a chopping-block mouth that might snap down on your fingers or come alive at night. It's just a simple V-shaped squeezer with a palm grip that crunches, snaps, and pulls apart.

The easiest ones to crack are the hazelnuts, round and small, followed by Brazil nuts, curved and dark. Sometimes the effort's not worth it. After breaking one of the nuts open and clearing out the debris, you discover it's rotten inside.

Dad lounges in his wheelchair and I sit on the couch, pretending to read *Bleak House*. Without taking his eyes off the TV, he says, "Where were you all day? I know you didn't go to school."

"How—"

"The front office called right before you got home. I told them you were under the weather. But that's the last time I'm going to do that."

I glance toward the kitchen. "Does Mom know?"

He pauses the TV and turns to look at me. "No. So. Where were you all day?"

Before this weekend, I would have lied. But we understand each other now. At least, better than we used to. "Took the train to Chicago. Just wandered around."

"You're not trying to run away?"

He and Hunter are obsessed with me running away. Where would I possibly go?

"No, I'm not running away."

Pecans are the hardest to crack open. Sometimes Dad uses an extra tool, a miniscraper, to pull out the hidden shelves that run down the center of the nut. The scraper looks like an instrument from an archaeological dig. You have to be careful cracking a pecan because the splinters could fly out, and everything inside the shell could break and crumble into bits of dust. To get an unbroken half pecan from the shell or, more amazingly, the whole piece, is a rare treat so I can't believe it when my dad's successful. Hunched over his armrest, fingers working carefully, he spends twenty minutes on his project and then sets five whole, perfect pecans onto a small plate.

"Go give these to your mother," he says.

Ever since he got diagnosed with diabetes, I stopped looking for things about him to respect and admire. His patience. His kindness.

I used to think Mom wasn't getting anything out of her marriage, and maybe it's still lopsided, but now I think there could be things going on in my parents' life that are hidden to me and Hunter. There are things we see and things we pretend we don't see, things we hear and things we pretend we don't hear . . . and things, I guess, that we never see or hear at all.

24

ON WEDNESDAY I SHOW UP FOR COUNSELING, BUT MRS. Hamilton doesn't let me in. She thinks it's better if Ricky and I see her separately from now on. What the hell?

After school I catch up with him at his locker. I'm dying to throw my arms around him, but there's like this force field between us.

"I got your e-mail," I say, lifting my paw in greeting. "Sorry I couldn't write back."

"Why'd you do it?" He gently holds my wrist in both his hands.

"Because you wouldn't."

He winces. Direct hit.

He peers under the splint. I know from similar excursions my hand's a purplish, sickly abomination.

"You're bruised," he says. "It means you're alive. The body can't bruise once the heart stops beating."

"How do you know that?"

"*CSI: Miami*, I think." We share a brief laugh. "All this, this hurt you're going through—it means you're alive and you have to stop wishing you weren't."

I swallow back my emotion. "It's not the same for you. You didn't do anything wrong."

"Can you go for a drive?"

I shrug. "Okay. I just gotta tell Hunter."

Ricky and I drive in silence for a while until I figure out where he's taking me: his old neighborhood, Lake Bluff, so we can look out at the water. You need a permit to park at the beachfront, and sure enough, in the corner of his car window, there's a sticker with the community logo. He pulls right up to the water, as close as he can get.

There's no moon, and it's dark all around us, except for streaks of dusty snow over black ice. The frozen lake is so peaceful. It's the calmest, most right I've felt all day.

"It's beautiful," I say.

"Sometimes when I stand on the ice, and I look down into the water, I wonder if I'm really under the ice, looking up."

"Deep." I smile and nudge his ribs with my elbow.

"You're really tough on people sometimes," he says. "Like your brother."

My smile drops. I tell him about Shelly and Hunter sleeping together, and he thinks about this for a second.

"People mess up, you know? But you can't see past it. It's like you choose one thing about them—the worst thing—and say, 'That's who they are,' and ignore the rest of it. Why not choose the best thing about them instead? Or the thing they do the most?"

"So you think I should thank Hunter for all the times he *didn't* sleep with Shelly."

"No, I'm saying that's just one thing out of a thousand. What about the nine hundred and ninety-nine times he's been a good brother, or Shelly's been a good friend?"

I don't say anything.

"I mean, do you know how many times my sister drove me to school when *she* was a senior? None. And then there's your dad. I know you hate that he's in a wheelchair. I get that, but—"

"That wasn't one thing. That was a hundred little things, over months and years, like choosing what he eats every day and what he drinks and whether he exercises, all adding up—"

"I know, and I'm sorry about that, but—I'd rather have your dad than mine sometimes."

"Don't say that. My dad's really sick."

"And you can't accept it. You can barely stand to be in the same room as him."

"Because this isn't how he's supposed to be. I just want my old dad back."

"But . . ."

"Is this why you wanted to go for a drive?" I mumble. "To tell me how much I suck?"

"No. My point is you're tough on other people, but you're toughest on yourself. What happened at the diner—the way it ended up wasn't your fault. And your heart was in the right place."

My heart. Right. That foreign thing in my chest I've been trying to expel for months now.

"You wanted to save the *gunman*. I don't know anyone else who would've thought about it that way," Ricky says, looking at me with something like wonderment. "But even if you think it was your fault, it's just one thing. It's not *who you are*. You're millions of other things. You're funny and beautiful and dedicated and athletic and smart, and you're a good teacher, and your students miss you, and you have this hard shell, but sometimes you let me see how sweet you can be, and I feel so special I get to see that side of you that you try so hard to protect."

He cups my face in his palms and kisses me, hard and loving, but I break it off.

"What's wrong?"

I stare down at my lap. I could take the easy way out and thank him for saying all those nice things about me, but soon enough we'd be back where we started—with me begging him to fight, and him refusing, and me never knowing whether I *can*.

I glance up at him and whisper, "I can't be with someone who doesn't take me seriously."

"I *do* take you seriously—"

"I'm small, or whatever, and I'm cute—you've said it a few times. But those words also mean I have no power, and if that's all you see . . . you'll never see me. Or at least, the person I want to be."

"I didn't mean it that way."

"I know it doesn't make sense to you, but the only way I know how to prove to myself that I won't freeze up again is to be in a fight. If you want to respect me, you have to respect the fact that I know what I'm asking. That I understand the consequences."

"One fight?"

"And you can't hold back. If you hold back, that's worse than not doing it at all."

"But what about your hand?"

"If someone's gonna pick a fight with me, they wouldn't care that I'm injured. They'd consider it an advantage."

He refocuses his gaze forward, onto the lake. "I don't know.

I just think one of us is gonna get hurt, and you've been hurt enough."

"Ricky, before I met you, I loved my friends and my family, but I think I loved teaching most of all. I thought I was making a difference, but I'm just passing on the same problem. How can I teach people how to defend themselves if I don't know how? How can I teach girls what to expect in a fight if I've never been in one? All my fights, every single one at the *dojang*, have had rules or time limits or a beginning, middle, and end, choreographed as much as one of Shelly's dance recitals. It's never been real. I need something real, or I'll never know. That's all I'm asking."

"But . . ."

I wait for him to continue. Even when he starts the car and puts it into reverse, I wait. I wait the whole drive home. Nothing comes.

Whatever he was going to say has drifted away. I guess the thought wasn't worth continuing, or maybe he didn't have anything to continue it with.

When he pulls into my driveway, he insists on walking me to the door. He looks so sad and earnest in his green-striped scarf and puffy jacket.

"So you don't want to be with me anymore?" he says.

There's nothing I want more, which is why I shouldn't have it. I don't deserve the things I want. I shouldn't be happy—not for a moment. All the time I've spent with Ricky was stolen from a dead man.

I dream my heart is a peach being eaten by rats until only the pit remains, wrinkled and tough, like a pecan.

Children's Home Rule number four: Children will maintain good relationships with their brothers and sisters.

What if you want to, but it's been so long that you don't know how?

The day before Christmas break, Mrs. Hamilton calls me and Dad in for a conference to talk about my grades and everything else.

I show up early, startled to see Grant Binetti slouching on the bench outside the counseling office, his backpack and skateboard at his feet. I wonder why he's seeing Mrs. Hamilton. Maybe I'm not the only one who got defeated by *Bleak House*.

I take a spot on the floor, as far away from him as possible. We've kept to ourselves in class lately.

The hallway's empty except for us and silent except for the soft ticking of the big clock outside Principal Simmons's.

"Where's your crony?" Grant says after a while.

"My . . . what?"

"Your crony. Your friend, the dancer."

"I know what a crony is," I say.

"I never see her around anymore."

"She transferred to a school in New York. A dance school."

"Oh."

Long silence.

"Does she like it?"

"Does she . . . ?"

"Does she like dance school?"

That's an excellent question. "I, uh, I don't know, actually."

"I didn't mean to push her that time," he says. "My friends shoved me into her; they were fooling around. I didn't mean to push her."

"Oh. Okay."

"Do you still do Tae Kwon Do?"

Before I can answer, Mrs. Hamilton sticks her head out. "Grant, you're up next."

I wonder how long he's been in counseling and whether it's the reason he never gives me a hard time anymore.

"Good luck," I say. It just slips out.

He looks surprised but recovers. "You too."

Dad arrives a few minutes later, wheeling up the ramp and through the automatic doors. Snow dusts his jacket and head, matting his hair down. He doesn't see me right away.

I watch him rolling himself through the hall, and I remember sitting in the police station waiting for him, watching him exactly the way I am now, and I think, this is my father.

This is my real dad.

He is in a wheelchair.

This is who he is now, and I will have to learn to love this version of him.

"The problem is Imogen is stuck," says Mrs. Hamilton. Even though I've been coming to her for months now, today she acts like I'm not in the room. She addresses everything to Dad.

"She was deprived of a fight-or-flight response at the diner, and the chemicals in her brain are still waiting to do one or the other. The continued denial of that response has made her anxious, scared, and depressed. This is common in children or teenagers who feel helpless. We've reached an impasse, and it's obviously affecting her schoolwork. She's failing English Lit and Current Events and getting Ds in everything else."

"Is it the same for Ricky?" Dad asks.

"Ricky has employed a different set of coping mechanisms. But as far as Imogen's concerned, I think we should keep moving forward, try to get to a place where she realizes it was an impossible situation she had no control over."

Wasn't that what I was trying to do with Ricky? Set up a fair fight on a level playing field to get it out of my system? Why can't she explain all that fight-or-flight nonsense to him? And what have his coping mechanisms been this whole time? They can't be weirder than mine.

She finally speaks to me directly. "I've arranged for you to visit with Officer Jenkins over break. He's set aside a half hour on the twenty-sixth to speak with you at the police station."

My nonheart vibrates disconcertingly, shaking back and forth like an elevator plummeting to the ground. I don't want to go back to the station. This is a terrible plan. Neither of them sees my panic, or if they do they're ignoring it.

Mrs. H. turns back to my dad. "When she speaks to Officer Jenkins, Imogen will learn, hopefully, that the situation in the diner was a distinct event that will not be repeated and that she's still a capable, skilled young woman and martial arts is still worth doing."

"She gets to start again in January," Dad says.

"I don't think I'm going back to martial arts," I say.

"What? Why not?" Dad protests. "You love martial arts."

But I don't even know if that's *true*. I loved what it gave me. And then I hated it for what it didn't.

Mom's upset about my grades. She thought I'd actually finished *Bleak House*. I don't know what could possibly have given her that impression; at one point the book's sole purpose was to help me reach the top shelf of the pantry.

"No one realizes how hard it was for me to get Bs and Cs before," I tell her, leaning against the fridge. "I worked my ass off."

She frowns at the word "ass" but quickly recovers, deciding that's a battle for another day, I guess.

"Why did you work your . . . butt off last year and not this year?" she asks.

"Because I had to keep my grades up for Grandmaster Huan."

"So you only did well in school so you could continue doing martial arts?"

"Basically."

"Maybe we shouldn't have pushed you to be in the class ahead," she muses. "Maybe it wouldn't be the worst thing if you redo junior year, at your own pace. Give you some more time."

"And be stuck at Glenview High for two more years?" I cry. "No. That's not an option."

Of all the years to relive.

"You're failing classes. You're clearly not ready to move on," she tells me slowly, as if I don't remember. "You're not mature enough to see the big picture."

"Right. I'm only sixteen. I'm practically a baby."

"No one's calling you a baby. I'm just saying maybe you would handle the sophomore material better."

Oh GOD. If I have to spend another year in that shithole while all of my friends graduate, I will seriously do something drastic. "Fine, so let me go do my homework."

Children's Home Rule number five: Children will do their homework in a timely manner.

Mrs. Richardson said if I fix my summaries and write five honest, thoughtful responses for the Current Events assignment, she'll pass me. Barely.

Summary of Article: In Dusseldorf, Germany, there's an old folks' home where the staff has trouble with confused Alzheimer's patients leaving the grounds and getting lost. To curb their disappearances and keep them safe, the town has constructed a fake bus station where patients can sit and wait for hours. It's a bus stop to nowhere. For each patient it represents a different place: home to their families, maybe, or to childhood, or a town that no longer exists. They wait all day, until they forget what they're waiting for.

What the U.S. Can Learn: We can be more innovative in the ways we treat senility.

Personal Response: I'm probably supposed to think this is sad and horrible for the patients, but don't. I envy them. They still believe there's somewhere they can go that will give them back all the things they've lost.

I don't resurface for dinner. I wait until cocktail hour: after Mom and Dad have gone to bed but before Hunter gets home from work. He keeps a spare key to the liquor cabinet in his sock drawer. I've never used it before.

Christmas break starts tomorrow, and I have no plans. Or at least nothing I'm happy about. The only thing on my schedule for the next few weeks is "Stop failing classes" and "Talk to Officer Jenkins." I'm afraid I'll have a panic attack just from being near him again.

If only Ricky could go with me to the meeting.

But Ricky won't be coming over to practice. Ricky won't be coming over at all.

The cabinet's in the kitchen at the back of the pantry, floor level, with glass and wood casing. I think it was a gift from Mom's sister. I've never paid it much attention, and I don't know the difference between the bottles, some of which are dusty, so I take out five and prepare a taste test, using Dixie cups.

"To freedom," I mutter sarcastically, toasting precisely no one.

The first drink's amber colored. It goes down so harsh it lights my eyes on fire; it's an oaky-wood sting that leaps up my throat to my nose. The membranes feel like they were rubbed in sandpaper and then slapped with disinfectant. Mmm, tasty. Alcohol: If you've ever wished you could drink floor cleaner, this Bud's for you. They're all pretty nasty, but the raspberry Stoli, which is half-full and looks clear as water, is the least nasty. Democracy: When you vote for the lesser of all evils. Why am I creating bumper stickers in my head? It sucks that Ricky's not here to hear them, that I'm the only one laughing at them because I'm the only person in the room.

I don't know how much you have to drink to get drunk. Five gulps? Ten? I place the bottles back except the Stoli, which is kind of small and fits conveniently in my coat pocket.

I put on shoes, a sweater over my pajamas, a heavy coat, and a scarf, and I creep outside. It looks like the whole world's had a pillow fight. Feathers of snow have drifted over every surface, coating the streetlamps and roofs, casting a soft glow as far as I can see.

"Good-bye, Mother. Good-bye, Father," I whisper. Children's Home Rule number one: Children will greet their parents when they come home, and say good-bye to them when they leave. (Nobody said they have to hear you.)

Stoli nestled securely away, I set out through the neighborhood, toward Glenview Martial Arts. The studio on the second floor is closed of course, completely dark, and looking up at it hurts my neck.

Grandmaster Huan was pretty crafty. He never had to hire a cleaning service, because high-ranking belts were responsible for keeping the *dojang* clean. After the last class of the night, we wiped the windows down with Windex and paper towels and pressed a soapy rag over the sweaty punching targets. Vacumed the carpet and put away all the paper cups for water.

He was running a business, and running it well.

I finish the Stoli and picture myself hurling the bottle at the largest window of the studio. But I can't bear the thought of Grandmaster Huan showing up on Monday and seeing that someone's desecrated his lovely school. Can't bear the thought of any little kids stepping on broken glass or feeling unsafe when they come to practice.

The school was my home. It made me feel like I could do anything. Every kid should get to have that feeling, even if it doesn't last.

I drop to the ground, on my back, and make a snow angel to protect everyone. The movement makes me nauseous, but I don't stop. Tears and snot drip down my cheeks into my ears. I wipe away the evidence with my sleeve.

When you pour water on a dead bug, it twitches out a final dance, just enough to trick you into thinking it's alive. That's how I feel, waving my arms and legs: unreal, like an imitation of a girl playing snow angels, like the rubbing of a gravestone, like a tracing-paper sketch.

When I was with Ricky, I felt solid. Without him, I tear apart easily. Is it the same for him? Is he lying somewhere in the snow on the other side of town, feeling the same way? *I'm sorry, Ricky. I'm sorry.*

I black out, and when I come to, there's vomit near my feet, and my pants are wet. Not from snow.

It all seems so familiar: the ruined clothes, the stench, the sticky skin. Like this has happened before, and it'll keep on happening until I get it right.

When I stagger home, the lights are all on. At first I think of beacon lighthouses in a storm, guiding me safely over the rocks. Then I think we're overcompensating for our lack of Christmas decorations. Then I realize everybody's up, waiting for me in the living room. I stumble through the door and flop down in the hallway, pleased to be lying down again, cool, smooth, comforting floor, where the world doesn't spin as much. I'm stinking up the place, waiting for the cops to cut me out of my clothes. How many pairs of pants will I ruin this year?

"Where have you been?" Mom cries. She's in a housecoat and one boot, a mug of coffee in one hand, clearly about to Search Party me out.

"Do you know what time it is?" Dad croaks, swiveling in his chair to face me.

"She's plastered," Hunter groans, throwing his hands up.

Mom's by my side in a flash, her eyes wobbly with fear. "What happened? Where have you been?"

"Nowhere, just down the street, Glenview Martial Arts." I burp.

"What were you doing there?"

"If the German grandmas can go back in time, I thought I

could, too," I say, which they chalk up to incoherent drunk-speak.

"Hunter came home and checked up on you, and you were gone," Dad narrates.

"You were in my room? What were you doing in my room?" I ask.

Hunter does this weird flailing dance of rage. "Are you serious? What was I doing in your room? Look what I found," he says, pulling a wrinkled pink piece of paper out of his pocket. He thrusts it at Mom. "I thought she was at this!"

It's the flyer for Kitty Kat fights. He dug through my *garbage*.

Mom takes it from him, unfolding the paper and looking at it. "What's this?"

"It's basically soft-core porn; they advertise it like it's a fight night for women, but I've seen the site, it's like *Girls Gone Wild*. It's disgusting," Hunter says in a rush.

"Oh, it's disgusting," I spit. "Like you don't look at worse things every day."

"You're sixteen!" he howls.

Mom squeezes my shoulder. "Did someone touch you? Did they hurt you?"

"Oh my God, that's not where I was! I've never been anywhere near it. I looked at it online, *once*."

Hunter turns his ire on Mom. "How can you guys be so oblivious? Dad barely leaves the house anymore, and you spend all your time trying to pretend none of this is happening!"

"None of what is happening?" Mom asks, sounding genuinely confused.

"Imogen having nightmares every night, sneaking out of the house, trying to get herself assaulted—I'm the one who has to deal with it. I'm the only one." He makes this frustrated half scream, and for a second it sounds as if he's laughing, but I know he's not. I've never seen him this upset before, not even at my birthday when Hannah called him out.

Hunter wipes a hand across his face and takes a deep breath, making a concerted effort to sound calmer, but his voice still vibrates with tinny anger. "It's been four months since it happened. I need to live *my* life now." He fixes Mom with a stare that makes him look way older than seventeen. "It's your turn. You guys deal with her."

We're all quiet after that, stunned mostly, and we just watch as Hunter walks up the stairs.

"I'm gonna crash at Adam's for a while," he says.

"Thank you for helping your sister," Mom calls weakly after him, but he doesn't respond.

Mom helps me through a change of clothes. I'm a ragdoll, incapable of keeping my head up or stopping my arms and legs from flopping about. She guides me back downstairs and settles me on the couch. Dad gives me a sleeve of plain crackers. I nibble on them and sip a mug of water and stare at Mom through tear-clogged eyes, at the hazy stained-glass image of her, as she sits down on the other side of the couch, as far away from me as possible. She's repulsed by me, doesn't want to be anywhere near me.

"Where were you tonight, and why did you get drunk?" she asks.

"I told you. I was at Glenview Martial Arts. I didn't go anywhere else. I swear."

"But you thought about going to this, this Web site?"

"Not really. I just wanted to be in a fight, where someone can really beat me up, and I can really beat them up."

"You want someone to beat you up?" Mom asks quietly.

"I want to prove myself. Show the world I *do* know what I'm doing, I'm not a fraud, that my black belt *means* something. I can fight, if someone will just give me a chance." I swallow tightly. "When I punched the mirror and cut up my hand, I felt relieved because now nothing bad could happen to me for at least a few days. I got a time-out."

"You think only bad things are going to happen to you?" Dad says.

"I think God will punish me if I don't do it myself," I whisper, staring at the carpet.

"I know it feels like your life will always be this way," Mom says, edging nearer, within striking distance, daring to put her arm on the couch behind my head. "But things will get better. You won't always feel this way."

"It's okay, it'll be okay, it'll be okay," Dad murmurs over and over, like he can't stop, like they're the only words he knows.

"No, it won't," I sob. "It wasn't okay for you, Dad. Something bad happened to you and that was the end. That was the end. I want to love you the way you are now, but if I do, that's like saying I'm okay with it. That I'm okay with you killing yourself. And I'm not okay with it. I'm not okay. I try to help. I try to get you to exercise, and I try to get rid of your junk food, but it's not enough . . ."

He opens his mouth to reply, but if he answers I don't hear it because I have to crawl to the bathroom to throw up again. I am a Japanese salaryman, puking on the train.

This would never happen to DJ. Her parents know everything going on in her life. I wonder what that would be like, instead of having a mom who never hugs you and a dad who doesn't care if he misses out on eleven years of his life with you.

25

I'M PRETTY SURE SOMEONE TOOK A NAIL FILE AND JAMMED it through my left eye in a botched attempt at a lobotomy. Smelling hurts. Seeing hurts. Hearing hurts worst of all, I think. This is my first—and hopefully only—hangover, so I'm no expert, but I think being forced to listen to carolers at 10 a.m. qualifies for the top ten torturous sounds the morning after.

Benign components of my room, like my sheets and comforter and window and lamp, have taken on sinister, otherworldly attributes. Turning over on my side requires monumental effort, and my stomach is so fragile, the tiniest shift could upset it again. Light, even the barest sliver under my door, is too much to look at.

I shuffle downstairs and open the front door to thank the carolers / shoo them off.

There's a white minivan in the driveway. Stenciled on the side of the vehicle is MIDWAY MEDICAL SUPPLY AND PHYSICAL THERAPY.

I pull open the garage gym door and see Dad sitting in front of the mirror. It's been fixed, and he's lifting ten-pound weights with his arms. A woman in her thirties with a stopwatch around her neck is spotting him.

"What are you doing?" I say, my voice hoarse.

"Imogen, this is Rachel. She's my physical therapist."

"Hi, Imogen, how are you? Do you remember me?" she says.

I wrack my brain for the answer. "I think so . . . from the hospital last year?"

"Yes. Good memory. I'm going to start working with your dad while you're at school. He told me a lot about you today."

"Oh." Does she know I'm still partially drunk?

"Would you like to see what we're working on?" She holds out her clipboard, and I can see a calendar with different schedules highlighted. "I made a copy for you, and I'll be back twice a month to monitor your dad's progress."

"Thanks."

"Well, I'll be seeing you around," Rachel says. "Have a good day."

After she leaves, Dad motions for me to come closer, and I do. I squat so we're at eye level.

"Your life is not over," he says forcefully. "It's not the end for you. Not even close. But it's not the end for me either. I like my life, Imogen. I know it's hard for you to imagine, and it's been hard for you to get used to, but I'm grateful to be in this wheelchair, considering what could've happened. I know I've slipped up the last few months; I was stressed over my book deadline, and I fell into old habits. Bad ones. I'm sorry I scared you. I'm sorry I didn't realize how much it was affecting you. But you don't have to try to save me anymore. Okay?"

Behind his glasses, his eyes look small but full of determination.

"Okay," I tell him, my eyes welling up.

"You don't need to worry about me. You just let your mother and me worry about ourselves."

I nod.

"You can have the garage in the evenings, but I get it in the mornings. Deal?"

He holds out his hand and I shake it. His grip is strong and assured, the way I remember it being when I was little and I trusted him more than anyone.

"I wish I'd been at your black belt test," he says. "I should've been there."

"That's okay. I could reenact it for you sometime. Once I'm feeling better."

"I'd like that." He clears his throat. "Can you hand me that towel?"

"Sure."

"Tell Mom I'll be in for lunch."

"Okay . . . Dad?"

"Yes?"

"I missed you," I whisper.

"I'm right here," he says. "I'm not going anywhere. I promise."

After lunch (plain crackers for me, soup and salad for Dad), the phone rings, another contender in the top ten torturous sounds the morning after. Mom hands me the cordless. "For you," she says.

"Hi, Imogen, it's Mrs. Alvarez. Ricky's mom?"

"Is he okay?" I ask immediately.

"He's fine. How are you?"

I want to laugh, but it would probably split my head open. "I'm okay."

"I know you're not really friends with Ricky anymore, and I know it's your holiday, but I'm in a bit of a fix or I wouldn't be calling."

"What's up?"

"I've got an outreach program scheduled for this afternoon at the women's center—a lesson on self-defense—and my expert canceled at the last second. Are you available?"

"I'm grounded, actually." (One of the few things I remember clearly from last night.)

"Do you think your parents would make an exception?"

They might, but it wouldn't matter; I can barely walk, and my hand's still in a splint. "I know someone who can help."

Taylor and her mother arrive an hour later.

"Thank you so much for doing this," I say.

"What does she need to do?" Taylor's mom asks. She seems young, and she wears a lot of eye shadow.

"Mrs. Alvarez will do all the talking, and her son, Ricky, will be there to help. Taylor, you remember Ricky—he was here on Halloween."

"Yeah."

"He's familiar with all the blocks and the basic kicks, so you can run through your three-step routines, from shoulder, collar, and wrist grabs. He'll move slowly, and he'll take his cues from you. Whatever you feel comfortable with."

"But how do I start?" says Taylor. "I've never done a demo before."

"Would it help if I show you the one I did at school earlier this year?"

"Yeah, that'd be cool."

We sit at Dad's office computer and I fire up the digital video of my demo. It hurts to look at, for more reasons than I can list, so I go to grab some water in the kitchen while they watch. When it gets to the part where Grant Binetti yells from the audience, I scramble to turn it off.

It's bad enough Taylor's seen me with a hangover.

They're running late to the women's center now, so I wish them luck, thank them again, and ask Taylor to let me know how it goes.

Once they're off, I shuffle back to Dad's office and hit Play on the video.

What I see onscreen is very different from what I remember. There's a fine line between confidence and arrogance, and I've crossed it. Maybe I crossed it well before that day in the gym.

What I see is a bully. Grant was rude and obnoxious and jealous, but wasn't jealousy kind of the point of the demo? Hey, everyone: look what I can do, and you can't! I was the bully, and I'm supposed to know better. Of course he couldn't break the boards; of course I would defeat him. Knowing that should've been enough for me. Instead, I wanted everyone else to know.

"Shut up, Grant. Why are you even here?" someone had shouted at him.

It's so obvious now. Why was anyone there who wasn't my friend? Because they liked martial arts and wanted to sign up for lessons. Grant was always roughhousing in the hall, pretending to be a fighter, and he went to see a martial arts movie the night I was at Cinema 8 with Hannah, DJ, and Philip.

He was going to sign up for classes. He was interested in joining the school, but I crushed it out of him. He could never sign up after that, not when he knew he'd have to see *me* there.

I grab the phone and frantically stab the numbers to dial Taylor's mom's cell.

"Hi, it's Imogen . . . Can you tell Taylor something for me? Tell her the most important thing—the most important thing at her demo—is to follow the rules of white belt. No ego, pride, or conceit. Tell her the most important thing is: Don't make anyone else feel foolish. Okay? Thanks. Thanks."

Ever since Hunter's epic freak-out Mom's been sleeping in my room on a futon, like a seriously messed-up sleepover.

While she's at work during the day, I hang out with Dad.

"I'd like to paint my room," I tell him after breakfast. "Can you take me to Ace Hardware?"

He's taken aback. "Right now? Today?"

"Yeah."

He thinks for a second, glancing down at my hand in the splint. Maybe he's picturing me holding the paintbrush with my teeth. "Let me call and see if they're open."

....

Dad helps me pick out colors. I don't mind that it takes the minivan wheelchair lift forever to lower in the parking lot. I don't mind wandering around the big, empty store and waiting for clerks to load up the paint for us.

I cover my carpeting with plastic and use my uninjured hand to paint the part of the wall farthest from my bed. I choose images from the summer, a stripe of aqua for the public pool, a block of forest green for Shelly's car, and lush blood-orange and yellow shimmers for the sky at sundown. I don't expect anyone else to recognize the shapes. It's more about a feeling to hold on to until the feeling comes around again.

When I'm done with the first wall, I take a picture on my phone to show Dad downstairs, and he says he likes it a lot.

"You really don't have to do this," I tell Mom on the third night as she settles into her makeshift bed on the floor. "I was okay when you and Hunter went to DC."

She gives me a look that says, "Don't even try."

"I wish you'd told us you were having so many nightmares. It hasn't been fair to him. It's not your fault; it's mine. But it hasn't been fair."

"I know."

As usual, she pulls out a paperback to read, but I want to keep talking. I roll sideways on the bed, prop my face up with my elbow on my pillow. "Did you have sleepovers when you were a kid? What'd you do at them?" I ask.

She puts her book down, considers my question. "Well, we played 'light as a feather, stiff as a board' and truth or dare."

"Let's play truth or dare," I say, sitting up and kicking my legs back and forth so they hit the mattress. "Want to?"

"Okay, but no prank phone calls," she says with a wink. "People can trace that stuff now." She and Hunter are so alike sometimes it's eerie. I'll never be able to make winking a part of my repertoire of expressions.

"I'll go first. Dare."

"I dare you to go back to Tae Kwon Do," she says.

"Mommmm. You have to dare me something I can do right now."

"That's my dare."

"We'll see," I tell her. "I haven't decided. Your turn."

"Dare."

"I dare you to paint something on my wall."

"Like what?"

"Whatever you want. Something nice I can see from my bed."

"Hmm. Probably not tonight . . ."

"Okay, then I dare you to run around the block in your pajamas, in the cold, for all to see," I say.

"No way. Truth."

"You already said dare, and you already deferred one!"

"What're you, a lawyer?"

"Come on."

And she does! I can't believe it! I cheer her on from the window as she makes her mad dash around the block, arms propelling her forward. I let her wear boots and a hat, but the rest is her flannel pajamas. She runs fast, too, and I dart downstairs to open the door for her when she gets back. Her nose is pink and she's totally winded.

"Go, Mom!" I say, holding my hand up for a high five.

She indulges me and then places her palm on her chest, taking some deep breaths. "Brrr," she shudders. "If I get sick, you have to make me tortilla soup. Get the recipe from Ricky's grandma."

Once her breathing resets, we go upstairs, and I know it's just going to be truths from now on. Which is okay with me.

"My turn," I announce. "Truth."

"Have you ever smoked cigarettes?"

Ha! This is what keeps her up at night? Cigarettes? Then again, there's not much left to choose from. It's all kind of happened.

"No, blech," I reassure her.

She nods, pleased. "I tried them when I was sixteen, and I felt the same way. Yech."

"Your turn. Truth?"

"Mmm-hmm."

"How come you never hug me?" I ask, and it's like all the air's gone out of the room.

She frowns, sending wrinkles throughout her soft face, especially her brow, like one of those cute pug dogs.

I take a long breath, but not so anyone would notice, a trick I learned in martial arts. It's important to breathe out in a short, forceful burst at the moment of impact when you're punched. Mom tries to clear her expression, smooth it over with an invisible rolling pin, but I've already seen how the question makes her feel.

"I've been trying to," she says eventually. "You always move back when I try, or make a face. When you were a baby, you were the same way; you couldn't stand being held, you struggled in my arms until I set you down so you could crawl away."

She's talking for herself, now, not me.

"I remember being surprised because Hunter was the opposite: he always wanted to cuddle as a baby, and he would grab on to my legs when I had to go out. Neither one is better," she's quick to add. "Just different."

I remember her teaching Hunter how to swing dance when he was twelve, so he could show off at the seventh-grade winter formal. They were in the kitchen with the radio on, laughing and twirling and knocking into the countertops. She and Hunter belong to a family where people are friendly and outgoing and happy, where they wonder how they got stuck with people like me and Dad.

"If you hug me now, I promise not to move away," I offer.

She looks at me and smiles, then gets up and tentatively puts her arms around me. Most awkward hug of all time. I stay very still, to prove I'm not gonna freak out, and then I hug her back, burying my face in her soft neck. She smells like the snow and her skin is chilled, but I feel warm and loved, like I belong to that parallel family she has with Hunter, like I've always belonged, and I hold on tight.

When I wake up the next morning, a new painting on my wall greets me.

A beautiful rendition of Monet's water lilies.

26

WITH HUNTER AT HIS FRIEND ADAM'S THE PAST FEW DAYS, the house has been quiet. Maybe we should get used to it; he'll be off to college in a few months and the three of us will have to deal.

Children's Home Rule number four: Children will maintain good relationships with their brothers and sisters.

But what if one of them has left?

On Christmas Eve day, I get checked out by the doctor, who removes my splint and tells me I'm healing nicely. I can grip a pen now and write really sloppily.

I think about texting Ricky the good news, but it's not fair of me to contact him. I'm the one who broke things off.

Hunter shows up in time for dinner. He was gone nearly a week, and he looks better now. Well rested.

"Greetings, Brother," I say with a shaky smile. My Children's Home Rule.

"You okay?" he asks me.

"Thanks to you," I say.

He nods, shortly.

For Christmas, I get three *Bleak House*–related items. I wish I were making that up. CliffsNotes in my stocking, the Scully-from-*X-Files* version on DVD, and a download of the Books on Tape edition for my iPod. I'm surprised the freakin' Chipmunks don't have an adaptation. My family claims they made these purchases independently, but I smell a conspiracy.

There are also plenty of Christmas cards under the tree from relatives and friends of my parents. Grandmaster Huan and all the kids at Glenview Martial Arts sent me one, too. Grandmaster wrote, "We are very excited to have you back in January."

I go through the cards again and again, wondering why there isn't anything from Shelly. She hasn't sent a single postcard from New York. I could write her an e-mail asking how she's doing, but if she wanted me to know, she'd have sent a postcard by now. I bet life in New York is amazing; she probably went skating at Rockefeller Center and saw the huge Christmas tree.

But I don't blame her for forgetting about me, especially since we'd barely made up when she left.

The day after Christmas is my meeting with Officer Jenkins. I go to the bathroom three times before we leave the house because I'm petrified I'll have to pee just from walking into the police station.

Dad assumes he'll be going in with me, but I need to do this by myself. I ask if he doesn't mind coming back to get me in a half hour.

"Are you sure?" he says.

"I'm sure."

I take my time, slowly winding my way up the stairs to the station.

In the lobby, Christmas and Hanukkah decorations are strewn about and there are garbage bags overflowing with Styrofoam cups and tattered wrapping paper leaning against the wall. They didn't even get yesterday off, but maybe they had a little party between shifts. I remember reading somewhere that incidents of drunk driving and domestic violence go up around the holidays.

I picture the cops' families at home last night, sitting around a fire and opening stocking gifts, all the while worrying about their spouses or moms and dads being on duty.

I have trouble taking my coat off. I shouldn't, because I have use of both hands now, but my arm is stuck in the sleeve and I wriggle self-consciously, trying to fling the damn thing off, when someone comes to my assistance: it's the female cop who looked out for me last time I was here. She holds the back collar of my jacket in place, which allows me to tug my sleeve off.

I swallow and hang my jacket on the hook.

The female cop is looking at me. "Tough year, huh?" she says.

I nod. I don't trust myself to speak without crying. Not because I'm sad, but because she's so kind. It's the smallest gestures from a stranger that get to you sometimes. "Thanks," I whisper.

"You're here to see Officer Jenkins, right? He's running a bit late, but he'll be here soon. Take a seat wherever you like."

I nod again and perch on a chair. When I thought I'd be getting this over with immediately, I felt okay about it, but having to wait has thrown my self-assurance out the window.

My nonheart is frozen solid, unmoving, so the pulse points in my wrists and throat are amplified. I pick at my lip and stare at the clock.

My pulse points and I sit there for ten agonizing minutes before Officer Jenkins arrives and leads me to his desk.

He's younger than I remember, maybe in his thirties, and slim but hard, like he has a lot on his mind. His short, choppy brown hair has gray flecks mixed in; maybe the gray is a recent addition.

He drinks a glass of water like he wishes it were a beer, and then he seems kind of at loose ends, like he doesn't know what to do with his hands. He rests them on his knees and then clasps them awkwardly in his lap. A badge sits on his desk, but he's not in uniform. Just plain pressed pants and a button-down white shirt, rolled up at the sleeves.

I feel small in the chair across from him. I'm glad he's not wearing his gun holster.

"We're a lot alike, I think," he says. "We both want to help people. My objective that day was to keep as many people alive as possible. I wish it'd gone down differently, but what's done is done."

I'm not sure what I'm supposed to say. I don't even know the difference between a sergeant and a detective.

"Mrs. Hamilton said you already have your black belt. Which explains the shiner I got last time we met."

My face feels warm and pink. "Sorry about that. Sorry." Should I have brought him Dunkin' Donuts as an apology?

"I didn't get my black belt until I was twenty-six," he says.

"What martial arts did you take?"

"Some judo, hapkido, karate. It helps me when I have to cuff people, get 'em in the car."

"But you still carry a gun," I point out.

"It'd be great if no one did, but the criminals do, so I have to, too."

"Is it true if you hurt someone and the cops find out you're a black belt, you can get in more trouble?" I ask, thinking of my laminated ID card with my full name and photo.

"Sometimes. It's called excessive force. If you do more than you need to in order to subdue someone. If you go overboard."

"So why doesn't it work the other way? Why don't I get in trouble for *not* doing something when I should have?"

He leans in, propping his head up on his hands, his eyes squinting slightly as he regards me. "It's not that simple."

"But he wasn't going to shoot her, was he," I point out. It's not a question.

"No, I don't think so. But we can never know for sure. He was high, he was unpredictable, he was pointing the gun at anyone and everything, including us."

"What did it look like, when I got out from under the table?" I ask. I think I have everything pieced together, but I want to hear it from his perspective.

"He raised his gun, and he pointed it at you. We yelled at him some more and moved in closer. He turned the gun on us, on three armed officers, and that's a death wish. Have you heard the term 'suicide by cop'?"

I shake my head.

"It's a way to die without . . . It's a tactic. He had a history of risky behavior, of reckless disregard for his own safety. And he had options, but he didn't take them."

"He wanted to die?"

"Looks that way."

Suicide is selfish, I think. After you do it, everyone else has to go on living, only they'll never be the same. His parents . . . his friends . . . do they know it was suicide?

"If I had kicked the gun away, tripped him, *anything* before he saw me there, he would still be alive."

He hesitates. "Maybe. Maybe not."

"And maybe if he was still alive, he could've gotten better, he could've gone to rehab, he could've gotten off drugs."

Jenkins looks dubious. "Maybe. I'm not sure he wanted to get better. And you can't . . . put it on yourself. *He* chose to commit a felony. *He* chose to carry a deadly weapon. *He* chose to put your life, the cashier's life, and my officers' lives in danger. I have a family. They have families. And you're just a kid," Officer Jenkins says, kind of gruffly.

I can see in his eyes that the decision weighs on him, and I'm certain now it was his voice I heard. *Light him up.*

"There were three police officers in the room. You know how many people are responsible for what happened?" Jenkins asks.

I don't answer.

"Four," he says. "Daryl, and the three of us wearing badges.

That's all. We tried to talk him down, talk him into putting the gun down, but when we got the right angle, we felt we had to take it. Do you think you can understand that?"

I offer him the tiniest of nods. "I'll try."

A crack forms in my ice heart, thawing it to a temperature that allows it to beat again.

When he gets up to shake my hand, he bows, and I return it.

Dad picks me up right on time, and I ask him to drive me to the cemetery. We ride over in silence, no sound but the heater blasting. The silence feels comfortable, though, not charged with the usual awkwardness. He's in a wheelchair, but he's still Dad, and I don't care if he walks again as long as he fights to stay healthy and strong.

He wonders if I want company, but I'd rather go alone. It's the second thing I need to do by myself today.

My boots crunch through the thin layer of snow that's settled on the ground. My footprints are the only ones around, winding along a path that seems to have no clear direction.

I'm not going to monologue to Daryl's grave like we're friends. I'm not going to throw myself to the ground and make a scene like a widow draped in black.

I just want to acknowledge my fault in what happened, and I'm pretty sure I can do it in two words.

27

HUNTER DRIVES ME TO HANNAH'S FOR NEW YEAR'S. MOM and Dad have plans and don't trust me by myself at home, so they asked Hannah's parents to babysit. Hannah still thinks we're heading to Gretchen's party, so when we arrive, she calls us into her room, where she's twisting her hair into a complicated pattern and making a crownlike circle at the top. I can tell by Hunter's wide, hopeful eyes and abrupt lack of conversation that he likes what he sees.

"Want a pop or anything before we go?" Hannah says, and then to me, "How come you're not dressed up?"

I see a golden opportunity to make things right with

Hunter. It gets pretty sappy, so here are the CliffsNotes. Expect a quiz at the end.

Me, to Hannah: "I'm grounded. Your parents are going to watch me."

Hannah (looks down, starts to undo hair): "Well, then, I shouldn't go to the party either."

Hunter: extreme sad eyes.

Me: "You guys should go together."

Everyone: Gasp!

I drag Hunter to the corner. "Go," I tell him quietly. "Have fun. Text me photos."

"Why are you doing this?"

"Because I love you, and I want you to be happy, and I'm sorry for turning your senior year into shit."

He whispers in my ear, cupping his hand over his mouth like we're kids making fun of Grandpa's snoring. "Thank you."

The next few hours are a bit surreal. Hannah's parents, who are kind of old, serve Triscuits with Brie and watch the ball drop *twice* in Times Square—once at 11:00 p.m. and a second time at midnight in reruns. They offer me sparkling grape juice, but anything resembling alcohol disgusts me, fruit flavors in particular. I don't want to spend my night celebrating another city's New Year, so I thank them for having me, wish them good night, and head upstairs.

I lie in Hannah's spare twin bed and stare at the ceiling. I remember lying on my back in the garage gym and staring at the ceiling that time with Ricky when he asked if I had a boyfriend, before we'd kissed or anything, when kissing was nothing more than a frightening and exciting possibility.

I wonder what Ricky's up to tonight. Is he having a good time? Was he able to leave the house and have dinner somewhere? I hope so.

Before we broke up, I'd planned on buying him a new pair of sneakers for Christmas.

I miss his voice. I miss looking into his eyes and holding hands and kissing and being treated as if I'm precious or fragile, even though we both know I'm not. It was still nice being treated that way sometimes. It was nice being thought of as special and worthy of attention and affection. Being vulnerable with another person can be terrifying, and doing something terrifying, even though you're scared, is brave.

I'll never be the kind of person who kisses on the first date or has a one-night stand, and that's my choice. But there's nothing wrong with wanting someone to hold you or dance with you at a New Year's party. There's nothing wrong with feeling good. It doesn't make you weak. It doesn't ruin relationships or make them cheap.

I don't like what Hunter and Shelly did, but I understand why they did it, especially Shelly. She never gave herself permission to have fun outside ballet or outside her friendship with me. She was always on schedule to be a performer, never allowing herself to have crushes or go on dates or be a regular teenager, and then she was afraid she'd be ostracized at dance school, so she tried to catch up with everybody in a single night instead of letting things happen naturally over a period of time. Maybe she went overboard, but I should never have made her feel bad for wanting to kiss someone, wanting to have sex, or wanting to enjoy herself. I guess I was scared of losing her, or of being forced to do those things, too, before I was ready.

At home the next morning I type an e-mail.

> January 1st.
>
> Hey, Shell.
>
> (Not a nickname we ever use.)
>
> Hi Shelly,
> Hope New York is amazing and you're having fun in school.
>
> (What am I, her mother??)
>
> Hi Shelly,
> Hope New York is amazing and dance classes are going well.

Just wanted to check in. I haven't heard from you since you left, which I totally understand because NEW YORK!! but I wanted to make sure it's not because of me not apologizing right. I'm sorry I ignored you. I get now it had nothing to do with me and that I overreacted. Hunter is actually not so bad a choice. I forgive you and I hope you can forgive me one day, even if I don't deserve it.

Love, Imo

I click Send, and then I look up the Manhattan Dance Company online and find a calendar that lists all of Shelly's upcoming performances with the Juniors Program. Then I call the florist that's closest to her school. They're not open, of course; just because I've decided to start fresh for the new year doesn't mean everyone else has. I try 1-800-Flowers instead.

"Hi, is it possible to preorder flowers to be delivered backstage every opening night? It'd be one this month, two the next month, and two the month after that."

"Yes," the person at the other end replies, "but I'll need a credit card and preauthorization form filled out."

I check with Mom about using her card, and I pay her back for the first delivery with Grandma's Christmas money. The rest will come from my allowance.

"How do you want to sign the cards?" the florist asks me.

"Keep it anonymous."

It's not about me getting credit; it's about Shelly knowing

she's loved. It's about being the friend I should've been when she lived here. If she figures out it's me, cool; maybe she'll see I'm sorry, and not just about Hunter, and not just for now. If she doesn't figure it out, that's okay, too.

Next thing I do is call Hannah and ask how the New Year's party was. She got home after I was asleep, and I left in the morning before she woke up.

She and Hunter didn't kiss at midnight because everyone blared noisemakers instead and it would've been weird. But he held her hand all night and opened doors for her and junk, so I tell her if she wants to, she should invite Hunter to the Valentine's Day dance. It's a month away but you have to plan early because it's ladies' choice and there's a system.

A week before the dance, girls have to compose a valentine to the guy they want to ask, but they don't sign it. The poem's a clue. If the guy knows who sent it, he can approach her and say yes. If he doesn't know who sent it or he doesn't want to go, he just won't respond.

Last year, Hunter got seventeen valentines.

It was a school record, a point Hannah immediately throws in my face. "Why would I set myself up to be one in a hundred?"

"Because I'm going to help you, and because he's been pining over you since my birthday when you told him off."

She giggles then, a telltale sign if ever I heard one. "He only likes me because I don't like him. This'll wreck it."

"But do you like him a little bit?" I wonder. "Confess; I won't get mad."

"Fine, a little bit—but I like being pursued even better."

We compose her poem:

I may not be there when you call
I may not buy a dress at all
You're lucky if I dance with you
When Cupid lifts his stupid bow
'Cause if you were to ask me out
The answer would be No.

On January 4, I get an e-mail from Shelly.

Subject: postcards

Imo,

Thanks for the note. I don't understand why you haven't gotten my postcards? I've sent AT LEAST five to you, and five to my mom! That is so weird. I'm late for class but I'll write more later and try to re-create all the things I said in my postcards.

Love, Shelly

P.S. Hannah e-mailed me out of nowhere and asked permission to take Hunter to the V-day dance. I told her to go for it, and I meant it, but what the fuh? I thought she hated him more than you do.

I call Mrs. Eppes and she's like embarrassingly thrilled to hear from me, so I feel bad for cutting to the chase, but I need to figure out what's going on. She hasn't gotten postcards, either, which is even stranger than me not getting any; it's unlikely Shelly wrote *her own address* wrong. Maybe the ink was smeared on all of them, making them impossible to decipher.

I re-read Shelly's e-mail and the thing that bothers me most is the P.S., the words "hated" and "Hunter" in the same paragraph.

The rest of January flies by. Grandmaster Huan calls a few times, but I'm still not ready to go back.

Instead, I focus on Children's Home Rule number nine: Children must study their schoolwork at school and at home.

In February, the Monday before the Valentine's Day dance, when all the girls deliver their poems to the guys they like, I linger in the hallway after Ricky's counseling session so I can talk to him. Something's clicked into place for me, about what my dad said in December. *You don't have to try to save me anymore.*

I think I know why Ricky's been going to separate sessions with Mrs. Hamilton. The diner didn't affect him the same way it affected me, because we were part of two different stories. In his, he saw a girl under a table who was about to do something dangerous.

When Ricky steps into the hall after counseling, I tell him he was right that day we first stood outside Mrs. Hamilton's office and he said I got the worst of it. What I need to know is how he got any blood on him at all.

"Why'd your shoes have blood on them? You were too far away," I say. "You shouldn't have gotten any blood on you."

"I was right behind you. I could see what you were gonna do, and I tried to stop you."

We stare at each other and I know that he loves me.

He's been trying to stop me ever since.

"You don't have to worry about me anymore," I tell him. I lightly touch his hand. "I mean it. I'm going to be okay."

He closes his other hand around mine, protecting it between both of his, the way he's been protecting my heart.

Was he dating me as a way to control the situation? Was he hanging out after school and doing fight club so he could know what I was up to at all times and make sure I was okay?

Even if he was, I don't care. I just want him back.

After we separate, I slip my folded poem into his locker.

I don't have a heart that's red

I have a heart that's black and blue

And if you land a single punch

That heart belongs to you.

At dinner we beg Hunter to read his valentines aloud. He's shattered his record from last year, which isn't a huge surprise. Seniors get the most valentines because they have all four grades gunning for them, whereas nobody sends cards to the grades below them; it's tacky to pan for gold in towns nobody's vouched for.

Of his twenty-one cards, two are X-rated drawings instead of poems, ten are fairly normal variations on "Won't you be mine?," one is a threat ("You *will* be mine"), one is totally desperate, four are from previous dance dates (unacceptable), one is shockingly eloquent—constructed in true iambic something or other (A TEACHER?), one is from Hannah, and one is creepy and illegible.

He plucks Hannah's poem from the stack and slides it over to me. "Recognize that handwriting?"

I pretend to scrutinize it. "Maybe."

"Tell Hannah to put her hair up the same way she did at New Year's," he adds.

I grin. "Tell her yourself."

"So it *is* her!" He grins back, triumphant as a lion that's brought down its first gazelle.

That night I dream I'm in the dressing room at Glenview Martial Arts getting ready for class. Everyone's lined up and they're all waiting for me, but I've forgotten how to tie my belt.

28

ON SATURDAY, THE DAY OF THE DANCE, I HELP HUNTER pick which tie to wear, and then I go outside for a walk. The sun's out for the first time in a while, so I head to the park. I've just stepped onto the melting grass when I'm shoved from behind.

"Ooof." I roll to the ground, tucking my head and using the momentum of the fall to rise to my feet and spin toward my attacker.

And that's when Ricky Alvarez punches me in the face.

My cheekbone blows up to the size of a fist, but I block his second punch and duck his third, getting in a jab of my own that connects to his shoulder.

He circles me, both his hands up, exactly the way I taught him, so they're protecting his face but not obscuring his view. I block his roundhouse kick, but he nails me with a sidekick that knocks the wind out of me. Once again I land on the grass, slowly aware that I can't breathe, that there's no breath left in the entire universe for me to access.

"Nice. Kick." I cough out, gasping to replace all the air I've lost. I stand on jittery legs, and my own hands come up. We're circling *each other* now, mutual prey.

I duck and weave, slide and counterattack.

My body hums with pleasure.

I kick.

I punch.

I swing.

I block.

I give as good as I get.

In our Valentine's Day dance photos, we look like kids from insanely abusive homes, except for the fact that we're smiling so wide, with aching teeth, matching black eyes, and puffy faces. I also have a bruise on my stomach the color of jaundice and the shape of Ricky's sneaker.

The important thing is that my hand, the one I broke punching the garage gym mirror, is completely unscathed, because when Ricky slammed me from behind, I reacted the way Grandmaster Huan taught me: tucking my head in and protecting my hands by making sure I didn't use them to break my fall. I absorbed the impact by rolling along my forearm and shooting to my feet.

When it counted, when I wasn't expecting any kind of fight and there was no gun involved, my training kicked in. My training worked.

Ricky gave me that.

He also proved I'm a good teacher. That's why his sidekick was so powerful; he twisted one hundred and eighty degrees when he executed it, exactly the way I taught him, so the full force of his body powered everything right through his leg and foot.

I didn't take the easy way out and kick him in the nuts or anything. I blocked his punch, pulled him in, and delivered a knife-hand strike to his throat that made his eyes roll back. When he came at me like a bull, trying to lift me over his shoulder, I darted out of his way and nailed the back of his knee.

He begged me to teach it to him next week.

Now our bodies feel pulverized and tender, but we hold each other up and sway on the dance floor. It even hurts to make out, our swollen, double-size faces rubbing together like jagged rocks as we kiss.

"Ow," we groan, going back in for more.

People give us a wide berth; no one wants anything to do

with us because we look like total freaks. DJ and Philip gape at us, so I take a page out of Hunter and Mom's book and wink back.

It was too late to join Hunter's limo group, but we're heading to Dairy Delight with everyone after.

The funny thing is, Hunter and Hannah have absolutely nothing to say to each other now that she's not making fun of him, so they spent the evening with other people. Hunter danced three songs with Gretchen, and I'm pretty sure I saw her pinch his butt. Ewww.

"Can you keep a secret?" says Hunter the next morning when we're alone. Mom's off running errands and Dad's working out in the garage. I've got a smoothie ready for him in the fridge when he's done. We don't keep junk food in the pantry anymore.

"What's up?" I ask, limping over, still way sore from the fight.

"I've decided not to go away for college next fall. I'm still *going* to college, but probably part-time, and probably at Glenview Community."

I'm stunned. "I can't believe you don't want to leave."

"I love it here. I love the lake in winter. I love going to football games in the fall. I love working at Dairy Delight. I love helping coach Little League in the summer . . . I love the park, the fountain, the—"

"Okay, I get it. You heart Glenview."

"I've been working at Dairy Delight for a year and a half now, but instead of having them pay me with checks, I had the Petersons hold on to my money for me. I've got enough to buy stock in the store and rent an apartment next year if I want."

Huh. So he wasn't lying about never having any cash. "Have you told Mom and Dad?"

"I'm waiting till after graduation. But here's my plan. Remember that night we surprised you after the movies and had that party for you to cheer you up, with the music from the concert in the park, and everyone was dancing?"

"You say party; I say disaster. Whichever."

"Oh. Really? You thought it was a disaster?"

I fight the urge to laugh, because he looks so shocked. I can tell this is important to him, so I quickly add, "It was a nice party. I just wasn't ready to be around people who'd been at the diner. But no, it was good, the dancing and music. So I get what you mean."

"Well, that's where I got the idea. I want to be a co-owner of the store someday and organize bands to play gigs. I think we could update the artwork, too, showcase students and local painters once a month. I'm gonna ask Mom to curate for me. Think she'll go for it?"

"I bet she'd be psyched," I say, thinking of her trip to the Art

Institute. "I mean, after she gets over the disappointment that you're not going to her alma mater."

We hear the front door open so we shut our traps.

"Surprise," says Mom, coming in and plopping a bunch of mail onto the table. "The post office called. They were holding six postcards from Shelly, all marked insufficient postage. They couldn't send them back to her because there was no return address. So I paid the missing amount and here you go."

"Hunter!" I yell. I dive into the cards, frantically organizing them by date so I can read them in proper order. "How old were the postcard stamps you gave me?" I demand.

He's annoyed. "I dunno. Stop shouting."

"Wild guess," says Mom, her amusement betrayed by the sparkle in her eyes. "Might they be ten years old? Might they be the ones Grandma gave you so you'd write her from camp when you were eight?"

"Maybe, I don't know," Hunter says. "Aren't they still good?"

"You dumbass." I laugh, turning away so he won't see me smile, so he won't see how happy I am that he's going to be around next year. Besides, I get the feeling he already knows.

With Grandmaster Huan's permission, I bring Ricky to observe a class at the end of March, so he can see if he wants to take lessons. He plans to join the Marines next fall, but he wants an official color ranking before then.

When we walk up the steps and enter the hallway, I feel a familiar stirring in my chest, almost like my heart's returned. Almost like I'm home.

I thought the *dojang* would feel different, but everything looks the same as it did before. The bright, spongy red carpet; the smooth, solid wooden bar along the wall. The motivational phrases and the corkboard with the school calendar and the belt test requirements seem frozen in time. The shoe bench in the hallway is tidy and organized, all the shoes facing the same way. The air conditioner's blasting even though it's cold outside.

Chief Master Paulson is teaching, and Taylor's wearing a yellow belt. I wait for her to finish saying good-bye to her friends before walking over. "Good job today. You were awesome."

She looks guarded. "Does this mean you're coming back?"

I shake my head. "No. But Ricky wants to start lessons. Can you look out for him? Give him some pointers?"

She smiles shyly, shades of the Taylor I first met. "Sure."

I hand her my teddy bear, the one with the black belt, and I leave Ricky to chat with Chief Master before the next class starts. I walk down the hall to Grandmaster Huan's office. His face lights up when he sees me.

"Imogen, how are you?"

"Good, sir, how are you?"

We bow, and then he pulls open his desk drawer, takes out

my black belt certificate and photo ID, and lays them on the desk.

"I been expecting you sooner," he says, eyebrows raised. "Why you not come in January?"

He motions for me to sit, and I do. He pushes my black belt materials toward me, but I don't take them.

"I'm still failing English Lit," I say. The only thing Santa's twisted and evil *Bleak House* stocking stuffers did was make me resist the book further. Mrs. Hamilton thinks I'm deliberately sabotaging my grades so I won't be allowed back to Tae Kwon Do.

"What about other classes?" says Grandmaster Huan.

"Mostly Cs."

He nods. "And no bad behavior? No suspensions?"

"No bad behavior. No suspensions."

"Good. You can come back. Start today?"

I hesitate. "The thing is . . . I think I might have gotten my black belt too early."

He sits now, too, looking confused. "You are my top student."

I try to choose my words very carefully. "I'm not sure that's enough for me."

He cocks his head, curious. "What are you saying?"

"Do I still have six months free, because of the demo? Because of getting all those new students?"

"Yes, six months free."

"Can I transfer them to someone else?"

"Transfer?"

"Give them to someone else to use."

"You don't want them?" he asks.

"I'd like to give them to someone else."

I think about giving them to Ricky or to Taylor. But they're already committed; they'll find a way to be here, so I write down a different name for him. The name of someone who may have given up. Grant Binetti.

"I'll send you his phone number, and you or Chief Master can call him," I say. Maybe Grant won't take the call, or maybe he'll say no. But if he's seeing Mrs. Hamilton, he deserves that chance.

Grandmaster Huan picks up the paper and studies it and studies me.

"I hold on to these for you," he says at last, placing the evidence of my black belt back inside the drawer. "Maybe you change your mind."

"Thank you, sir. For everything."

I bow to Grandmaster Huan and shake his hand, and then I walk back into the hallway to stand next to Ricky.

We watch the start of the next class, the call-and-response drill.

"What is the Tae Kwon Do Student Creed?"

"I will improve myself mentally and physically, sir!

"I will respect my elders and teachers, sir!

"I will always defend the weak, sir!

"I will prevent unnecessary fights, sir!

"I will be a champion of freedom and justice, sir!"

Those words are tattooed on my brain; I'll never forget them. But I know now they're something to aspire to, not something you can always expect.

Before bowing, sitting for meditation, and starting warm-ups, classes begin with leg stretches. The low belts sigh and grumble to themselves, making Vs with their legs and grimacing as they try to reach their toes.

The high belts are completely silent, killing themselves for full splits, for that perfect line, because the heart is a muscle like any other.

Tearing it down is the only way to make it stronger.

EPILOGUE

I MADE IT TO ANOTHER SUMMER.

I even got my driver's license, which I needed because my new martial arts school is fifteen miles away.

I wanted to go someplace nobody knew me.

Dad helped me research all the local schools and all the different styles of self-defense.

Today is my first lesson.

I still want to teach someday. I want to teach girls to spar without gear. I want to teach them how to react quickly, think on their feet, and take a punch, so if someone ever hits them or gets in their face, they won't go into shock.

But all that is a long way away.

There are times I still go over it in my head. The diner. I picture different scenarios, imagine things I could've done, things the cops could've done; but most of the time I don't really see how it could've gone differently. Not anymore. It was up to Daryl.

I wish he had opened his hand—just opened his hand and let go of the gun.

I park the minivan, walk into the school, and take off my shoes. I bow to my new instructor, and she introduces me to the other students.

There are no colors on the wall.

I open my hands to receive my white belt.

I open my hands and let go.

ACKNOWLEDGMENTS

Thank you to my agent, Sara Megibow, for her optimism, encouragement, perseverance, and general wonderfulness. Thank you for celebrating all the small moments (and the big ones, too).

Thank you to my editor, Maggie Lehrman, who made this novel infinitely better with her fantastic insight. I think you knew the characters better than I did, and your edits allowed them to become their fully realized selves.

Special thanks to Dr. Caitlin Thompson, a clinical psychologist who does vital work counseling veterans. Your time and expertise in authenticating the PTSD elements of the book were invaluable.

Thank you to everyone at the Nelson Lit Agency for making my dreams come true: Kristin Nelson, Anita Mumm, and Angie Hodapp.

Thank you to the team at Amulet Books and Abrams Books for Young Readers, including Susan Van Metre, Erica La Sala, Jason Wells, Maria T. Middleton, and Angela Gibson.

Thanks to my family—Mom and Dad Hoover, and Rachel Murphy—for filling my childhood with a love of books, theater, and radio plays, and always supporting my creativity. Thank you to the Skiltons for giving me a second home and always reading and asking about my work.

I started writing this book in 2009. Many friends read early drafts, shared helpful comments, and/or offered me constant encouragement over the years: Amy Spalding (forever grateful to have found a kindred spirit with whom I can spend nine hours talking while wandering through Koreatown), Kristen Kittscher (sharing the pub journey with you has been so wonderful), Heidi Aubrey, Kirsty Wright O'Callaghan, Natalie Bahm, Miranda Kenneally, Sarvenaz Tash (samesies!), Juleen Woods, Stephanie Sagheb and the rest of the S'n'B ladies, and my smart and lovely cousin Anna Jay, who provided the coveted teen perspective. Thanks to Chelsea Valenzo Duggan, Jennifer Aynilian, Becki Jo Mack Miranda, and Kiana Brown Davis for your support and friendship in childhood, high school, and beyond.

Thank you to the Writing Night peeps, Team Megibow, my Amulet Sisters, the Apocalypsies, the Lucky 13s, and the Layas for making me feel like I'm never alone. Thank you to Cecil Castellucci for starting Pardon My Youth at Skylight, and for that pep talk when I needed it most.

Fun fact! There really is a hospital in Germany that constructed a fake bus stop to prevent Alzheimer's patients from wandering off. Thank you to reporter Harry de Quetteville, who wrote an excellent article about it for the *Telegraph*.

Thank you to my martial arts instructors in Libertyville and Los Angeles.

Lastly, thank you to my husband, Joe, my best friend and the love of my life. You helped inspire this story. Your sidekick that time in Kenpo when we sparred was really good (the flowers and ice cream after class were nice, too).

READ ON FOR AN EXCERPT FROM SARAH SKILTON'S NEW BOOK

THE EX BEFORE THE EX

I WASN'T INVITED, BUT I SHOWED UP TO THE PARTY ANYWAY so I could talk to Ellie Chen and find out why she dumped me two weeks ago. It was a choir party at Maria Posey's place, in celebration for killing it at the state qualifier yesterday, so I figured Ellie and her songbird friends would be there.

I didn't figure they'd be mixing it up with my new crowd from soccer and my old crowd from, well, whatever it is Ryder does these days.

I parked a few blocks away and walked up the hill, shivering. It might've been cold outside, and it might not have been. I couldn't tell anymore. Palm Valley, California, is just another place that disregards the seasons. It was January, but that didn't mean anything.

I was only cold because I remembered what it was like to be warm; the year I'd spent with Ellie was the warmest of my life.

When she moved here from New York, I could tell right away she was different. She was smart in a way that didn't make you feel stupid, and beautiful in a way that didn't make you feel ugly. It was like by having those things, and being that way, she made everyone around her believe they were more and better, too.

Now I drank to keep warm.

For Christmas, Granddad had given me his antique flask. The real present was inside, refillable every time I visited him at the hospital. He didn't need to bribe me with booze, though. I liked the old guy and I would've shown up every week no matter what. I liked his vintage magazines and I liked sitting and talking with him at Lancaster Medical while he recovered from pneumonia. Sometimes we'd just play cards and let the hours pass. Unlike my parents, he talked *to* me instead of over me.

The conversations I had with my parents didn't seem to require my presence.

Outside Maria Posey's million-dollar tract home on Western Avenue, I toasted Granddad and sipped my Christmas gift, wincing at the taste. The San Gabriel Mountains were oppressive dark outlines against a gray, smog-choked sky. They practically disappeared on nights like this, but I could still feel them there, separating me from Los Angeles and Pasadena and all the other places that might've been worth living in.

I'd just stumbled through Maria's doorway when my first ex, the ex before Ellie, slithered toward me out of nowhere and looped her arm around mine.

"It's been a month, Dix. You gotta let it go," Bridget said.

"Two weeks and four days," I corrected her, scanning the crowded living room for Ellie. The air was charged, and a few sets of eyes found mine and squinted in curiosity or disapproval. It was hard to tell which.

"It's not that kind of party," Bridget said, wrapping her fingers around my flask and lowering it out of sight between our bodies.

"It is for me," I said.

The hallway and kitchen were packed, too, and I considered mosh-pitting my way through, but Bridget tightened her noose of an arm around mine.

"Don't make a scene. Hang out with me instead," she said. Her large green eyes were like emerald caves, so huge a guy could stroll right into them and stay forever if he didn't mind giving up his own mind. According to Ellie, emeralds had a tranquilizing effect. Screw the Ramones—I didn't want to be sedated.

Bridget leaned against me and I glanced down to where her curves seemed to be inviting my hands on a date. I kept my expression neutral and forced my gaze back up to her lips, which were full and dark and red. Her strawberry blonde hair fell in loose curls over her shoulders, and she smelled like a dream, lush and harmless, but I knew better.

Whoever coined the phrase "girl next door," intending it to mean sweet or innocent, never met Bridget. We used to be tight, but she hadn't given me the time of day in years. Her sudden affection made me suspicious. Just like her emerald eyes, it was too good to be true. You can always spot a fake because it has no imperfections.

I shook her loose and staggered through the living room, dodging couples perched on couches or sprawled on the floor. The room swayed, like the house had become unmoored. I half expected to look out the window and discover a black ocean because we'd all been transported to Semester at Sea. But the floor moved only for me.

Everybody was talking about college admissions, scholarships, essays, and financial aid. Maybe that's why I hadn't been invited: my future was set, while theirs were still in flux.

I fought for balance and caught snippets of deadline-this and deadline-that, all while scanning, scanning, scanning for Ellie.

A couple of my soccer teammates (Patrick and Josh) gave me the nod, or maybe they were indicating heads-up, because suddenly Maria Posey, hostess and head songbird, stepped into my path and scowled.

"Why are *you* here, *Charlie Dixon*?" She threw her words like darts, apparently believing people's names could be used as insults. Or maybe just mine could.

"The beckhams are here, Ellie's here. I'm the epicenter of that Venn diagram," I slurred, and poked her on the shoulder to make my point.

She was disgusted, either by my breath or by the fact that I'd brought math to the party.

"Are you drunk?" she demanded. "I don't want you vomming all over my parents' carpet."

I didn't dignify that with a response. "I just want to say hi to Ellie, okay?"

With a last name like Posey, the pressure was on, but as always, Maria met the challenge. She struck a good one: hip cocked, hand out, eyebrow raised. It was quite a balancing act. I wondered if she'd practiced it in front of the mirror before guests arrived. The Velvet Rope, she could call it.

"Invite?" she demanded again.

"Must've gotten caught in my spam folder."

"Spam folders don't spontaneously generate invites. You didn't make the cut."

"Ellie's here, so I can be here," I pointed out.

"She broke up with you last year."

"Last year was a few days ago!" I took a deep breath. "Two seconds, okay? Then I'll leave."

Her eyes narrowed. "Fine. At least serve a purpose and sign my petition while you're here."

"What's it for? To ship you off to Vassar early or something? Give it."

"It's to convince Principal Jeffries to let the girls' choir perform at graduation."

Ah, graduation: the collective obsession of my classmates—save for me, of course. When you know exactly where you're going, the future holds little charm.

Maria handed me a stack of papers, and I indicated for her to turn around so I could sign it against her back.

When that was through, I found myself alone in the kitchen, turning in a circle, debating which exit was most likely to lead me to Ellie. Should I go back and retrace my steps? Or forge ahead in a new direction?

A Hispanic girl passed through on her way to the living room, her long, dark hair almost obscuring her large, hollow eyes. She looked like a sad girl in search of a tragedy. I could steer her toward mine, but it would cost her a finder's fee.

The sad girl and I glanced at each other. I didn't recognize her and we hadn't been introduced, so I didn't say a word. Every year it gets harder and harder to tell freshmen and sophomores from upperclassmen, and it's not worth the risk engaging them to find out.

I watched her leave, then spun some more—retrace steps, or forge new path?—until someone called my name. My oldest friend, Ryder.

"Hey," he said. An unlit cigarette dangled from his mouth, and he fiddled with a box of orange Tic Tacs, rolling it up and down his knuckles like it was a coin and he was a bored magician. "Didn't expect to see you here."

He was more out of place at this party than I was, and we both knew it. "Ditto," I said.

His dark hair was just long enough to tuck behind his ears, and it stuck out a little from under the ratty, knitted black cap he always wore. His eyes were bloodshot, his nose a little red, and his T-shirt had holes in it, but he still looked like a jock—albeit a jock who'd accidentally dressed himself as a stoner.

He shrugged. "I'm a sucker for songbirds. I'm sure you can relate. Gonna win the game on Friday? Agua Dulce." He drew the "l" out like taffy.

"That's the plan."

He didn't say anything else right away; just looked at me with an expression I couldn't read, empty as an ashtray in a house of former nic addicts.

"I'm heading out, but let's grab lunch on Tuesday. Off-campus? Find me if I don't find you." Ryder walked out the front door before I could answer.

I nodded anyway, and the floor lurched sideways as I wobbled toward the balcony.

Ryder had two inches and thirty pounds on me and he could've played varsity in just about any sport, but he'd failed the drug test freshman year, and failed to care all the years after that. When I met him the summer before sixth grade, he'd been all-American wholesome in his Little League baseball uniform, a star with limitless choices, limitless directions.

As if in deference to his former capacity for greatness, the party had rearranged itself to let him pass, so the direction he'd come from was now an open path for me, too, straight out to the balcony.

I tipped my flask to lap up fresh courage, and when I lowered it, there she was, standing outside in the windy January air, her back to me, in a face-off with the moon over who was more fickle.

A guy stood next to her, leaning against the railing, speaking intimately in her ear. The balcony wrapped around the side of the house, giving them plenty of room, so why were they standing so close together, arms touching?

"Ellie," I shouted.

The guy jumped and stepped aside: Fred from English class, looking frail and pasty like a good debate team nerd should.

Ellie turned around and stared at me. I stared back, dehydrated and dizzy. Her skin was smooth and pale. It reminded me of a cup of milk slowly being poured right before someone yanks the glass away. I was so thirsty, and she was just out of reach.

Her hands were small and tense at her sides, like doves waiting to be released into the air. Her silky black hair was pulled into a loose bun, held together by a lacquered stick with gold Chinese characters painted on it. A few loose strands framed her forehead. She wore a little bit of eye makeup, just enough to prove she didn't need any. This was the "Natural Look" magazines always advise women to go for, but no girl can actually pull off. Unless they're Ellie.

I wanted to cup her face in my hands and give her a kiss hello. Her lips were wonderfully soft looking; they never left a mark on my face, almost as if she'd never been there at all, and now I realized I wished she had. Worn lipstick. Left behind some evidence that she and I had really happened.

"What are you doing here, Charlie?" Her voice was soft and low and disappointed, so soft I had to lean in to hear.

"Your brother told me where I could find you."

A smile tugged at one corner of her lips. "He always liked you."

"Funny thing," I said. "You used to like me, too."

"I still do," she said, sounding hurt.

"Can I talk to you for a second?"

"About what?" She backed up and knocked into the railing. I covered the distance between us, but not too close, never too close.

I'd waited a year to ask her out, and on our first date I knew she was too good for me, but I pretended I didn't know, and I spent the next eight months waiting for her to come around to it, too.

Two weeks and four days ago I had agreed to meet her at Café Kismet for a cup of coffee. I came with a basket of pomegranates, her favorite, picked fresh from the tree in Granddad's backyard.

She showed up with a tired, regretful expression and broke it to me gently. But she never told me why.

I sat there long after she left, till closing time, unable to move. There were plastic Christmas lights hanging all over Rancho Vista Boulevard, mocking me with their cheer while my coffee turned cold, then bitter. When I got kicked out of the café, I walked around for hours without going anywhere, just so I wouldn't have to go home. I walked until the lights spun and blurred and flickered in my wet gaze like real candles. I walked until every single one gave up and blinked off, gone as if the desert wind had blown them out.

I could think of a million reasons for her to ditch me, but I didn't know *her* reason.

"You said hi. Now you need to leave," said Maria, tugging on my arm. She'd been head songbird since sophomore year, no small feat, and she ruled the other girls with an iron fist. Most of the time. Rumor had it there'd been a power play at the state qualifier in Pomona yesterday, but between whom I didn't know.

"I'm talking to Ellie," I snapped. "I don't *need* to do anything."

We'd drawn a crowd; I could sense a group forming a half circle behind me, but I didn't care. I wasn't leaving till I got a straight answer, nontourage be damned.

"Not here, not like this," said Ellie. "We'll talk later, okay?"

Between her and Ryder, people were lining up to talk to me later. Trouble was, I wanted answers *tonight*. "Just tell me why it's over," I begged.

She glanced at our audience, uncomfortable. "You changed," she said.

"How did I change?" I said, daring to inch closer.

"Well," she said, "for one thing, you started drinking."

The flask was not helping matters; it weighed heavy in my hand even though it was nearly empty.

"I only started drinking because you left me. That's not the reason." I moved closer, contemptuously. "Is it because of him? Are you with *Fred* now?" Maria was right; names could be used as insults, so long as they had the right target.

I gave Fred a quick push against the railing.

"Charlie, stop," Ellie cried, and I backed off, hands up and open, my flask gripped loosely by my thumb and forefinger.

I redirected my attention to her. "A *lincoln-douglas*? Really? After *me*?"

It was a lame-ass move, and I knew it. Even in my booze-addled state I knew it. Our school traffics in labels, but that was never Ellie's currency.

She was looking over my shoulder; she was already done. "Bridget, would you take him home? He's not safe to drive."

Unbeknownst to me, Bridget had followed me to the balcony, and she happily accepted the task. "Told you not to make a scene," she purred in my ear. "Keys?"

"You're not driving me anywhere," I spat.

"Charlie," said Ellie, stepping toward me and holding out her perfect palm.

I handed them over, and she walked past me, past the rubber-neckers and into the kitchen to place my keys in a dish.

In the passenger seat of Bridget's Chevy convertible, I dialed Ellie's cell and poured my heart out until her voice mail cut me off. I redialed, and it said her mailbox was full. I chucked my cell onto the backseat and banged my fist on the dashboard and generally had a little fit.

When I was done, Bridget was staring at me with her big cave eyes.

"That was the craziest voice mail I ever heard."

"Be glad it wasn't meant for you, then," I snapped.

"I'm jealous, actually."

"Then you match the light," I slurred, pointing ahead.

"What?"

"Green means go. And I'm the drunk one?"

Wind shook the car, making Bridget clutch the wheel and struggle to stay in the right lane.

We have serious gusts of wind year-round. It's the distinguishing characteristic of Palm Valley, the daily traffic warning on the electronic billboards that light up the 14 Freeway. It'd be nice to see "Coyote Attack" or "Child Abduction" messages every once in a while instead, just to mix things up.

"High Winds Ahead" loses its luster once you realize the wind's never going to be high enough to carry you away and drop you someplace else, like on the other side of the San Gabriel Mountains.

"You better not vom in my car," said Bridget direly. "Especially not over Ellie Chen."

"Can I vom over your driving?"

"Smart move, by the way, giving Ellie your keys so you'd have an excuse to talk to her tomorrow at school."

"She already told me she'd talk to me."

Bridget gave me a look like, *You naive little boy.* "Suuuure."

We drove in merciful silence through downtown, past the civic center. The windows of all the buildings were dark, like eyes shut against the world. Maybe they were pretending they were somewhere else—different buildings in different towns, where perhaps the sun didn't shine as much, but when it did, it meant it in a way it never seemed to mean it here.

Bridget felt the need to reminisce about our past. "Ellie never thanked me, you know. Not even once."

"For what?"

"Teaching you how to use your tongue sophomore year."

"Maybe you taught me too well."

"What do you mean?"

"That's the only thing she ever wanted to do."

"You dated a year and you didn't have sex?" Bridget said.

"Eight months." I frowned. "You seem to know a lot about our relationship."

"I keep tabs on my exes."

"How? Alphabetically? Or is it like counting sheep?"

"You're funny when you're drunk," she remarked. "Funny and bitter. I keep tabs on the ones that *matter*."

"Aw," I said sarcastically.

Bridget was still running around the nostalgia track. "Charlie Dixon, soccer hottie. Why did we break up again?"

"You dumped me because I wouldn't put out," I reminded her.

"That's right. You weren't fast enough," Bridget said, and chuckled. "Hey, I just thought of something. If you and Ellie didn't do it, that means you're still a virgin." She reached over and ruffled my hair. I gripped her wrist and returned it to her lap.

"So?" I said. "She is, too."

Bridget smiled, slowly and deliberately. "You sure about that?"

"Knock it off."

"I hear Fred's a skilled orator . . ."

"You heard wrong."

But I wasn't so sure.

We reached the street between our two driveways. My heart was a lead ball, rolling downhill. I felt sick. What if Ellie *had* moved on? (Worse, what if she'd moved on *before* she dumped me?) I couldn't move. I was back in Café Kismet, paralyzed.

Bridget leaned over, all the way over, to undo my seat belt, and this somehow involved her breasts brushing against my chest. Her lips hovered above mine. They were dark red, luscious, and wet. Unlike Ellie's, they would definitely leave a lipstick mark.

"Come inside? For old times' sake?" she said.

"Why so chummy tonight?" I wondered.

She was straddling me now and I placed my hands on her hips to keep her at bay. I honestly couldn't figure out how we'd gotten into this position.

"I waited a long time for you guys to break up," she said.

It was flattering to think she regretted losing me, but she was being awfully friendly for someone who hadn't bothered to wave back when I saw her outside her house last month. Something wasn't right.

"Well, this is my stop." I gripped her arms and tried to dislodge her without hurting her. "Can you, um, move?"

"Sure." She smiled devilishly and started a slow grind with her hips. "How's that?"

"Come on, Bridge, get off my lap."

"So I'm Bridge again, huh?" The swiveling continued.

"I mean it."

"Or what?" she asked.

If I couldn't have Ellie, I didn't want anyone.

"Bridge, Bridge, Bridge," I said, tapping her nose with each name, "I needed to learn with you so I could impress *her*. You were nothing to me but a *bridge* to Ellie." It was a dirty rotten lie, but it got the desired effect: she slapped me so hard my face burned. It felt like the perfect coda to a horrible evening.

At six a.m. on Monday, two deputies from the Palm Valley sheriff's department came to our house and said a girl named Maria Salvador had been dropped off at the Palm Valley ER a few hours ago.

She was alive but in critical condition, hallucinating out of her mind and speaking gibberish. She'd overdosed on LSD and entered a dissociative fugue state. They suspected she'd been given five times the normal dose.

Not surprisingly, her parents wanted answers. According to them, she never would have taken acid, or any other drug, voluntarily. Someone had drugged her. The best and only suspect so far was the dude who'd dropped her off.

Dad was confused, and asked the deputies how we could help. What he meant was, "Why are you here?"

The answer to his unspoken question quickly became known.

My car had been caught on hospital security cameras, dumping the girl and peeling away from the curb. It was then discovered in a ditch by the 14 Freeway. The license plate led the sheriff's department right to my door.

It was a frame job, clean and clear.

In my hungover sleep deprivation, I could only manage a few thoughts:

1. Who was Maria Salvador?
2. Would she be okay?
3. Why hadn't anyone tried to frame me for something sooner?

ABOUT THE AUTHOR

Sarah Skilton lives in California with her magician husband and their son. By day she works in the film and TV business. She is a black belt in Tae Kwon Do, which came in handy when writing *Bruised*. This is her first book. Visit her online at sarahskilton.com.